I never saw my father again. I could say that he was abducted, but no. I won't lie. He left on his own two feet, with the mathematician. That's what mother said, when they let her visit me in the clinic. The truck, my only evidence, disappeared with them forever.

H has come back. She looks back at me out of my bedroom mirror. But it doesn't hurt anymore.

Hate was invented here. In heaven, it doesn't happen.

out
of
the
cage

Out of the Cage

Fernanda García Lao

Translated by Will Vanderhyden

DEEP VELLUM PUBLISHING
DALLAS, TEXAS

Deep Vellum Publishing
3000 Commerce St., Dallas, Texas 75226
deepvellum.org · @deepvellum

Deep Vellum is a 501c3 nonprofit literary arts organization
founded in 2013 with the mission to bring
the world into conversation through literature.

Originally published as *Fuera de la Jaula* by Emecé Editores.
Copyright © 2014 Fernanda García Lao c/o Schavelzon Graham Agencia Literaria.
www.schavelzongraham.com
Translation copyright © 2021 by Will Vanderhyden

Support for this publication has been provided in part by grants from the National
Endowment for the Arts, the Texas Commission on the Arts,
the City of Dallas Office of Arts and Culture's ArtsActivate program, and
the Moody Fund for the Arts:

ISBNs: 978-1-64605-045-1 (paperback) | 978-1-64605-046-8 (ebook)

LIBRARY OF CONGRESS CONTROL NUMBER: 2021930868

Cover Design by Vic Peña | vics.work

Interior Layout and Typesetting by KGT

PRINTED IN THE UNITED STATES OF AMERICA

For G, my inverted me.

Years like moths erode internal organs.

Mina Loy

Aurora

1956

Point of the Arrow

The day of my death everyone was there. Winter had paused and spun around on itself like a tornado. It was a national holiday, I don't remember which one, but we were exultant. We'd stitched huge rosettes to our clothes, to the curtains, to our breasts. Our hearts pumped in bright bursts. And we laughed.

I loved those celebrations. The abundance in the attire, in the words, made me feel historic.

Yedra had ironed the boys' white shirts and suits. As a rule, they dressed identically.

Before going to the port, to commemorate the great forgotten deed, we filed out into the courtyard to sing the *Canción a la Bandera*, to honor the flag, which we raised at the least excuse. Our martial delirium no longer shocked the neighborhood. The tone-deaf ear of that nationless people had assimilated the trumpets and clamor of the battles we waged against amnesia, with the submissiveness typical of the cowering class.

That morning, the Colonel and I lined up in single file. He stood in front, not I. Off to one side, Yedra controlled the turntable. ManFredo, a little ways back, stared up at the sun or its opposite.

In the darkroom, Lana's gray eyes glowed in the shadows.

We sang facing north, a line with a twisted axis. Our bitter words and morning breath fell on the cold tiles. C'mon! I exhorted. But nobody paid me any mind. My family sang without zeal. The old glories sounded more and more watered down, more insipid. Only I sang with any intensity. I exaggerated the endings to show off my lung capacity. My gesticulations were over the top too. I kept time with my right foot, tapping to keep the beat. Otherwise the group would be lost. It's not easy to lead such deafness.

And yet, that day had been born for tragedy. In the middle of the line, *al purpurado cuello*, something unanticipated provoked my silence. And then, the fall.

Somehow, an LP, careening through the air like a demented boomerang, had severed my jugular. And I didn't understand who or what had thrown it. Maybe the bloody poetics of that line had become embodied in my throat. Bleeding, I said something nobody heard, as a clot of blood stained my dress. My pupils flashed, blinded by death, and I convulsed. My eyes stopped in midflight and fluttered unseeing, filled with images of the family who, oblivious, melted away like butter in a flame. They sang despondently on, imperturbable.

My death was so unexpected and exquisite that, for a moment, nobody noticed it. Not even me.

"Something's wrong with the *señora*," Yedra said, suddenly.

I teetered and the Colonel stood transfixed. Man covered his eyes. Fredo smiled like an opening cyst.

Domingo ordered Yedra to stop the turntable, spinning uselessly. The B side of the 1945 version of the *Policía Federal* had ended. Its notes still tickled my throat. That's how they finished me off. Patriotism hurts. A conscious and deranged cruelty lashes out against you.

"Suicide?" the Colonel asked, trembling.

"I don't know, I was adjusting my sock," Yedra answered.

Man looked to the left, Fredo to the right. Nobody, nothing. Just some plastic bags dancing suggestively along the wall.

A light rain fell and the Colonel began to cry. He'd gotten some dust in his eye.

They looked at one another, not knowing what to do. Finally, Yedra reacted and called Dr. Heine, who lived nearby. Nobody wanted to touch me. It was left to the doctor to remove the record from my throat.

Some dry lumps, invisible mortal scabs, stuck to the LP. If they'd put it on, the needle would've skipped at those protrusions of dead leukocytes. *Al purpurado cuello, al purpurado cuello.* But they would never want to hear my death.

The Colonel promised that the killer would be found, but the complexity of the matter kept him from the investigation. Without ever starting it.

White Lilies

Before the mortician arrived, they took my body into the darkroom. I couldn't figure out what they were doing with me. When the Colonel came in, the doctor withdrew. Yedra's grubby hands erased all possible prints from my body. She washed me with a cloth and I savored the sight of the soap mixing with my blood.

Then Domingo gave me a grateful look and got down to work.

"Leave us."

Yedra closed the door. Lana played dumb, holding her bare shoulder at a right angle to her dirty nose.

"She'll finally be good for something," she said in her thin little voice.

"Don't be so cold," replied the Colonel. "Lie down. I'm ready."

Those are the last words I heard with any clarity. After, words seemed to float underwater. That effect of immersion lingers. Hearing slips away, the world fades. I still see shapes, as if through glass. But death obscures.

The case was closed that afternoon. It was registered as an

accident to avoid attention from police or neighbors. Dr. Heine, who may or may not be a psychologist, came up with the idea.

The burial was quick. Closed-casket to keep the wound from being seen. Some of the Colonel's friends came by for refreshments and the courtyard filled up with garlands. The loveliest had a note that read, "From your friends at the committee." White lilies, purple ribbons of exquisite satin and gold lettering, from my *hipertensas*: the ladies of the Fulgencio López Hospital.

The last person to show up was Buda. She came in smoking a cigarette and caused a little ruckus, put to bed by the arrival of the cold cuts.

While everyone ate, she sat nervously beside me. Not pretending to cry. Everyone else had abused the system of grieving and now chewed fervidly. She watched the Colonel, the boys, Yedra inquisitively.

ManFredo stayed behind the divider, heads poking out one at a time. The General was there. When high command was in attendance, the *deformes* were kept in reserve.

Yedra served liquor and turkey tostadas. I would've preferred something else. But I couldn't move.

The Colonel seemed most affected. He said that he loved me, despite my character, my wanton past, and my mental coarseness. After dedicating a few overblown phrases to me, he proceeded, without interruption, to a discussion of springs. His favorite subject.

They didn't bring Lana out—that would've been too much.

The next day, they loaded me into a long vehicle, lowered me into a hole, and planted me there, in the dry earth. No tears, not one flower. Nothing to remember. I was a formality of no importance.

The Husk I Was

The priest spoke so quietly even I couldn't make out his words. Nobody paid him any mind, except Buda, who watched him with a frown. She moved closer to try to decipher his timid peroration.

"And Alba Berro has departed . . ."

My name didn't matter to him. The wind erases specifics, drowns out repetitious phrases, conceals apathy. Buda decided not to interrupt the priest; it was hard to catch what he was saying, frozen as he was by cold and a dearth of information. His little snout seemed to moan from inside his cassock.

". . . because death is a means and not an end. Those of you here, you must remember forever that life runs out, like a sin of the palate. The taste lingers in the spirit. Because the body is a bridge, not a mere hunk of flesh. In truth, I say to you: if you eat not the flesh of the Son of the Consoler and drink not of His blood, you shall have life neither in yourselves nor in Him. Alas for those of you who rend stomachs, hams, or heads with the despicable gluttony of the ravenous, you shall never sit at the divine table. For the church deems the sated ornamental seasoning, not souls in ascension."

His purple lips make you want to bite them.

"We are deeply saddened by the premature death . . ."

"Of Aurora," Buda said, suddenly.

"Pardon me?"

"My sister was Aurora. Not Alba."

"Exactly, and we share in your pain. Lord shelter her in Thine infinite bosom. Receive God, Aurora, the only wisdom, our Savior, who shall be your glory and splendor, empire and fortress, now and for centuries to come! Amen."

Everyone put on sad faces. The priest's words were strange. Yedra made as if to pray but stopped short.

Two workers lowered the coffin in silence. The one handling the side with my feet tangled the rope and my head thumped lightly against the wood. It reminded me of my mother's slaps.

ManFredo was the first to walk away, hands in pockets. Domingo and the rest of the attendees withdrew with a distracted air. The priest, overcome by a wave of nausea, curled up beside the next tomb.

Buda circled my headstone. She was furious. Seething with aggravation and repeating: Alba, please! Good grief!

I felt her pacing and stomping on the dry grass. But she didn't cry. Then, abruptly, she left. Almost at a run.

I lay stunned in my tomb. The minutes continued their sad passing and there I was—relocated. My consciousness detached easily and my vessel was all that was left, stiff and sinking. The husk I was threatened to go under.

That's how my life ended. With question marks. No certainties. For a time, I awaited my holy ascension, but it never came. The suspension of events would be the worst ending.

I returned home in a new state. Not solid, not liquid. Something like vapor, maybe.

I slipped in through a poorly latched kitchen window.

Terrible Repose

My death wasn't a topic of conversation, not even around the dinner table. Nobody shed any light on my murder while munching a legume. Neither the motive nor the author of the attack was an object of analysis.

That first night, Yedra prepared a chicken with an insipid side dish and nobody looked up from their plate. The bones were stripped to the rhythm of my family's teeth, in perfect harmony with my own.

That night, a deeply suspicious air of complicity prevailed. They all closed their doors without saying their prayers and limited themselves to silently sitting and tracking each other's movements. ManFredo wrote in his diary that my bad temper didn't justify my death. As if someone thought it did. As if someone believed that an irony of fate had ended my life by divine error or vengeance. A travesty. Somebody did kill me, but it didn't matter. Nobody cried, no death threats for the possible culprit. Everybody seemed occupied. Except for me, I didn't know where to put myself.

My only happiness came from my *hipertensas*. They came the next day and asked for a portrait of me. They wanted to frame it so I could preside over the committee's Room of Ceremonies. "A professional of suffering" was the phrase they used to describe me. Domingo promised an enlargement of my profile in black and white.

When they left, I wanted to go with them. But the house didn't let me leave. The enigma that keeps me here is produced within these walls.

I move through the house with the inconstant levity of my present state and finally settle in front of the vanity, to look at how it doesn't reflect me. Consciousness is a universal eyelid. When I shut my eyes, a new being will blink for me.

Fabulous Reality

I watch Domingo slip out of his room, with the stealth of a student skipping school. I already know what awaits him. Lana opens the door, revealing a bare leg, a moistening enticement. The false hero shuts himself in with her and, right away, her moans make me flee. They evoke what I am not.

ManFredo is asleep.

Across the hall, Yedra massages her calf, numb from age and poor circulation.

I'm overcome with something like sadness. I never imagined my absence would go so unnoticed.

The only visible change is that nobody goes out to the courtyard anymore. The flag will fade. It'll wither, hanging there, like a sock forgotten on the clothesline.

The Fatherland darkens.

Sharp Little Finger

I'm starting to forget things, but I still remember my name: Aurora Berro. I was the youngest daughter of a *tonadilla* singer who fled Spain during the war. When Mother came to America, she lost her stage and her husband all at once. Father disappeared at the port. He left the luggage, left us. He took just one parcel. I don't know what it contained.

We moved in with Mother's cousins and never saw Father again. And yet, I remember one afternoon on Calle Irala when a man with a moustache stopped and stared at me. He looked just like Father. Behind him, empty streets and the rain dancing on sheet-metal rooftops. Then, I forgot all about him. Life was nipping at our pockets and there was no time for nostalgia.

Sometimes we invited happiness over to dance in that desert. After washing the dishes, Mother put on a show of simulated joy in the courtyard, to the clapping of Italians and Poles who couldn't keep the beat. Buda, my sister, hated the enthusiasm of the flamenco and sat in her corner, with the dark face of one excluded.

I was the only one with anything resembling rhythm, a

bundle of nerves with waist-length hair who pretty soon was asked to come earn a little money. Growing up, I danced to pay the rent.

At fifteen my mammary charms and slender waist overshadowed my stiff legs and awkward kicks. I worked hard, but my body always lagged behind or ran ahead of the beat. Never quite coinciding. I didn't realize it at the time. But I see it now. My happiness was contagious, like leprosy.

One fine morning I woke up in the Alvear Palace Hotel, in the mayor's arms. I never knew his real name, but they called him El Roca. He was always hard, always coked up. A month later, the marquee above Calle Corrientes shone with my name and El Roca winked at me from the balcony.

He'd gotten me a part in a ridiculous spectacle, directed by a comedic capo and a dwarf woman with a black expression. I performed a boring little number, which quickly turned into the heart of the show. The dwarf would punish me and I would expose my private parts on the proscenium. She really whaled on me. And I displayed the bruises, my navel and neckline, nothing too explicit yet always enticing. The dwarf jabbed my bruises with her sharp little finger and the crowd went Ahh. Then, she put a drop of my blood in her mouth.

The house was packed for the macabre display. The reviews were devastating, but the fury that mad dwarf unleashed on my body was a hit at the box office. I ended up badly beaten but inundated with gifts. More finely wrapped all the time.

I moved to an apartment with a French balcony, surrendered to a man from Corrientes: Horacio Tabardi, El Roca's accountant. A strawman but of an exceedingly sensitive character. When a judge sentenced his boss to prison, he took care of me. Of the economy of my flesh. We threw ourselves into bed at the slightest provocation. But it wasn't love, or I suppose I would remember it better. Just lascivious surrender, no dessert.

Near the Alvear, I moved in with Mother, my sister, and a canary. An irksome little creature—a gift from the convict—that one winter afternoon I helped escape out the window.

I moved mechanically from my bed to the theater and from the theater to Tabardi. The rest of the city was foreign to me. Walking just ten blocks was enough to exhaust me. My body oozed juice, like a squeezed grapefruit. Up and down the stage. With Tabardi it was just the same.

Those were hard times. Mother and Buda would laze about the living room listening to jazz, eating imported cheeses, and barely speaking to me. I had performances Wednesdays, Thursdays, Fridays, Saturdays, and Sundays. I came home to the smell of tobacco and stacks of unwashed dishes. We argued all the time for no reason. Anything was fair game.

Buda started taking refuge in alternative religions. Mother got addicted to postwar cinema. In the last months, we only saw each other in passing at the bathroom. There was always a line.

Another memory, contiguous with the last, is, actually, just an image. The Colonel's inscrutable face in the elevator. He was our neighbor. I had no clue that open-mawed wolf would seal my fate. I was taken by his mustache. It was just like Father's.

The Enemy Advances, Bellicose Strophe

On our first date, Domingo took me to the movies. He chose the film. *Imitation of Life*. But as soon as that blonde actress appeared in the dark of the theater, he began to tremble. The situation aroused him. The starlet and her double. On a crowded beach and there beside him, sucking on a candy. He compared me to her constantly, his eyes welling. I almost missed the film.

That actress, one I was seeing for the first time, was his unattainable totem. His fallen virgin to be put back on the altar. That's why he was with me. I was a substitute. He saw a glimmer of her in me. "You just have to let her come out," he wrote in a notebook.

From that moment on, I became his object. To possess me, to transform me, and to worship my appearance would be his priority. And I had to quit the theater.

I didn't suspect the reason for his admiration. I thought I was special and unforgettable. Besides, the dwarf had worn me out.

Within a few months, Domingo and I were engaged. Fatally.

The accountant reappeared many years later. Mother spurned me.

"If you marry the sergeant, you'll be my enemy."

"He's a colonel."

"Whatever."

"And love."

"What love?"

"Yours."

"Irrelevant. It doesn't hold up to the slightest analysis."

"We do what is possible, we shall do the impossible."

"Don't come to me with little sayings."

"Marriage is vocation and discipline. Something you used to say I lacked."

"This is happening because you quit the show. Now your work will be to agree with your husband. A cur dressed as a colonel."

"I'll be a mother."

"Why bother. It's not worth anything either."

I never saw her again. To keep her from being right. For a long time she lived in El Roca's apartment and, later, she rented it out. I learned from Buda that she erased me from her address book. From her conversations too. She cast me aside like a stone.

Once, I thought I saw her at a funeral. I almost wept, but no. It wasn't her. The deceased shared her look of disgust.

She's not on this side of things. Not on the other side either. She had it in her to find a third time, just to prove me wrong.

Two Days Dead

Virginal state, mine. The initial unease has been replaced by a kind of hallucinated hyperobjectivity.

Deprived of body, I'm pure consciousness. There's no filter. I'm free of guilt, of love, of the pain in my back. I stop feeling anything. I am to one side of reality and it's so sweet to not participate, to be a witness.

And so I transcribe what I'm calling "Paranoid Vigil, or Postmortem Poetry," though I'm still not sure about that title.

Texts written in the air:

After fifteen minutes of being dead, jokes lose their humor. Fanfare fades, gets murky. When fantasy goes, hell is all that's left. Laughter can be grating.

Men with tasteless mouths, tasteless necks, tasteless laughs. Such are the ones I've known. Labyrinths lacking charm and gravity. My husband was a living fossil and my sons, hunks of matter of no ontological interest.

Curious monstrosity the moth—*mariposa nocturna.* Light and

instantaneous, flying its circular inspection, burning and ending. Like a death miracle, it has the gift of absence. It evokes fleeting images, inhaling cold and exhaling fire. Like me. Lacking any pleasure but the senses.

When anger is submitted to thought, it's just a construct held together by the pins of words. Refined hate needs to unleash itself and take its insolence on a stroll through real life. To break its neck against a specific being that will give it value.

To hate without a visible antagonist is a waste. A hysterical thirst, unquenchable. Pure vegetarian cannibalism. But to hate without body is a sin of omission: Lana, I hate you.

Nothing is more repulsive than to live marked by causality, or by cause/effect. The world has a logic that's denied us. To rely on chance or deduction is to take the easy street of madness. Madness and idiocy look a lot alike.

Despite consciousness, when you die you cannot write. Words lose meaning, turn into hollow sketches. You can only talk around them, in the corners of the house, after dark.

An exquisite loneliness takes hold of my hand and squeezes. The word is eternal.

The Colonel's Wishes

Now that I no longer am, I spend more time thinking about Domingo. As if I had the moral obligation to understand him.

He never wanted to be a soldier. He dreamed of battles less bloody. He was good with his hands. And he had unusual ideas. He disassembled all manner of machines with the skill of a surgeon. From early on he carried a screwdriver with him everywhere.

He could reconstruct an object, dissecting and modifying its structure, by studying its pieces carefully spread out on the rug. He wasn't all that interested in knowing the essence of things or in recreating them. He longed for their perfection. An increasingly subjective perfection, of course. All his own.

When he met me, he already had an assortment of differently sized tools, capable of disarticulating anything. But mechanics had saturated his spirit of curiosity. Everything ended up looking the same.

The first time he saw me half naked in the theater, he squeezed a little pair of scissors he always carried in his breast pocket. A reflex. He wrote it down in his notebook: "My hands betray my conscience. She's identical. I have only to dye her hair and sweep her off her feet. She will be mine."

That mission made him forget mechanics. He even stopped going to the movies.

Pinups of the unattainable object were compared to my photo in the show's program. We coincided in our small mouths, our hips, our feet, our eyebrows. And yet, I never had that sort of milky and sweet glow that she—the other—exuded. I was far more wretched.

In the beginning, learning English appealed to me. We went to class together. We ate an ice cream after. He pecked me with cold and sticky kisses. But when we got home, he insisted on lessons, late into the night. Sometimes he suffered furious outbursts at my bad pronunciation. I came to hate that language, his mouth. One night, razor blade in hand, I told him enough and he promised to let it go. We agreed that I'd just say *sweetie*, with the best accent possible. I never understood why.

The blond dye job gave me quite a seductive Ladino look. The men in the neighborhood drooled and the women snarled. We got married on February eighth. The birthday of Julia Jean Mildred Frances, the real name of the woman of his dreams, the one I was not.

For the civil ceremony, he dressed me in an exceedingly tight, short-sleeved sweater that made the judge and witnesses stammer. The church ceremony had to be postponed because the priest was having spasms. Two weeks later, we met at the altar and said a solitary "I do" without witnesses.

I wore a nondescript dress to not offend God. I expect I succeeded. If I'd known how I would end up, I would have done the opposite. Decency is pointless.

Copy of the Copy, Fraud

Today Lana brushed her hair with my brush, using a technique similar to mine. But with an odd twitch of the wrist at the end. Side effect, mechanical failure. It gives her a rare allure. Deformity is seductive. I just brushed my hair. For her, the brush coming and going across her head is a whole choreography. She extends the fantasy, to zones uninhabited. She's a perverse version that buries the original.

Domingo surprises her at my vanity and instead of scolding her shoves his tongue down to her trachea. She laughs. Her erotic capacity is immense.

I watch her suck and keep brushing her hair, unfazed. The Colonel's eyes roll back, as if looking behind him. She puts her hair up with my French clips, as a quantity of invisible semen stains her dress. My dress. Domingo was always of discreet ejaculations. Brief yet dense liquid.

The scene disturbs but doesn't discomfit. The tactile intrigues me. It might be this state of tormented zephyr that now defines me. I watch them like a movie, settling atop my perfume bottles to take in the porno of depravity, and discover a hint of compassion in the eyes of my incendiary past.

Domingo inserts his weapon in all her crevices, which spin like greased nuts. He fires with precision. Lana contorts and her spine quivers, the tautness of youth. They look like a bow and arrow, all in one. It makes you want to applaud.

If only I had a way.

Unattainable, Double

At the beginning of our marriage, I believed in happiness. The Colonel was scarce by day, dogged by night. We made his orgasms with great prolixity. After, we thought about him until he fell asleep.

But before long I observed that he knew the blonde's screenplays by heart. He repeated the dialogues in English over and over. When things got complicated, he was memorizing *The Strange Case of Doctor Jekyll and Mr. Hyde*, a somewhat affected production in which she'd given a good performance.

I'd gotten pregnant and was in an awful mood, my hips had widened, my face was swollen, my legs looked like sacks of flour. To top it off, the birth was terrifying, an all-out battle. There were children everywhere. The profusion of limbs knew no limit.

And so it was that my two-headed ManFredo appeared. We had to baptize them with a piece of name for each. I think nature imitates itself. ManFredo was the reproduction of the Colonel's burning obsession.

I got depressed and became anemic. I'm not sure which came first. What I do remember is that it was then that Yedra, the Colonel's distant cousin, first appeared. We hired her to look after the baby and right away she felt humiliated. She started calling me *Sacrílega*.

She was an expressionless and menacing woman from Tucumán. I could feel the hurricane stilled in her breast. Under the crucifix, the magma.

Meanwhile, my black roots and my weeping made cracks in my beauty. The Colonel was disappointed. I was moving ever further from his ideal. He began to maniacally sketch his blonde starlet. He recited entire speeches from her movies.

I didn't understand his words. I thought he'd lost his mind. He asked for leave and never returned to the service. He was thirty-six.

I never had time to love him, and when the *deformes*—as the neighbors called them—were born, I couldn't help but hate him. His monothematic obsession was disturbing. It made me feel like nobody. I took over the role of head of the household to make that clear. It was a blow that left him defenseless. Or so I thought.

A retired soldier is almost a civilian. In other words, a Don Nobody. I never forgave Domingo for not consulting me about his decision. I should have left him then. I should have donned my evening dresses and returned to the theater. Continuing to put up with all of that was useless. Maybe today I would be in a better position. Alive even.

Lana or Timbre

She has begun to roam the house. But she's clever, she waits until everyone leaves. She seems obsessed with my things. I discovered her wearing my pearls and my rings, singing along to my favorite music. And though she's off-key, her voice is powerful. It makes you want to weep.

If I were alive, I'd tie a knot in her vocal chords. Her little electric timbre reminds me of the canary. I want to open her cage, break her wings. Stew her. Sing from her mouth and say horrible things. But I can't. I follow her like a dog. Let my fury muss her hair.

Like a Lament

The Colonel took up photography and started taking group portraits. We opened a studio. The most distinguished members of the military milieu paraded in front of his lens.

I remember a towering captain with a diminutive wife. Domingo made them foreground the woman to distort her size. She no longer resembled an infant on a satin pillow, but a furious piece of fruit.

We designed beautiful backdrops to roll out across the studio wall.

Earth, Sea, and Sky—the military families immortalized their best profiles. Some of the photos even appeared in the newspaper. ManFredo helped with the fan. To make the fake battleship backdrop seem more alive.

I embroidered a felt sunrise with a warrior sun in a victorious pose that was quite popular.

I remember the day we decided to take a family portrait. The only one in all those years. The Colonel came out blurry. I was glowering. ManFredo was the only one smiling. His two parts agreed to be happy in front of the shutter. They posed with their heads lolling in opposite directions. Like an unbalanced scale.

I wept for hours when I saw that image. And I started to flirt with the idea of having them separated. They were still young.

In our social class, dissimulation is an inestimable value. A captain cannot bring out a mongoloid son in public, not even an asthmatic one. Even a low-ranking officer is capable of sacrificing his progeny if they're not up to snuff. There's a lot of zeal for reputation and appearances. An undiscerning wife is permitted, as long as she dresses elegantly and doesn't drool.

Though Domingo was retired, I still socialized with the military women. Women of refinement, with a penchant for vampirism or over-indulgence. My *deformes* offered fodder for their ghoulish murmurings.

"To rise in rank you have to make yourself loved by your inferiors and wanted by your superiors." So says the *Decalogue of the Good Cadet*. What a way to suffer alongside the pamphlet.

I always wanted to have one. A tall and rosy cadet, *en composé*.

Apologia of Hate

The ManFredos grew up ignorant of most everything. They thought their father harmless and me respectable. They knew nothing of my artistic past. The photos of my time as a flamenco dancer were carefully tucked away. I erased my life in one fell swoop.

And when they were school-age, I applied for an opening at Colegio Militar. Alone, I visited the Pavilion C dorms, the bleachers at the sports complex, the social club, and the chapel. I implored God that when I woke the next day, the ManFredos would be only one. The Colonel waited in the car. He looked inert, like a corpse. No expression of approval or its opposite.

A group of students were rehearsing their entrance for the officers' graduation. There were little flags and the smell of gunpowder. I lied to the principal, not mentioning my *deformes'* physical distortions. He enumerated the institution's benefits. He spoke of the tactical lecture halls, the shooting range, the indelible library, languages, physics, chemistry, the gymnasium and swimming pool. When I heard the words swimming pool, I fainted. I imagined the Manfredos in swimming trunks, turning their heads to breathe, wheeling their scrawny little arms like fans under water. The school nurse gave me a shot and left me in the infirmary.

We got the opening, despite Domingo. He didn't even contribute a smile. Or ask any questions. It was his way of expressing disagreement.

The first day of classes, I accompanied ManFredo. The sun hadn't yet risen in Palomar. It was raining. The entrance for new students was still locked. We waited on the sidewalk out front, partially hidden under an enormous umbrella.

Families began to arrive. Before long a chubby little boy started pointing at us. I can still picture his finger—a dark blood sausage aimed at us. Hundreds of perfect heads turned. There were hisses and muttering. The ManFredos could think of nothing better than to wave. They were still unaware of the gravity of their appearance.

The door opened and nobody went in. A slightly older boy approached us. He pushed aside the umbrella and burst out laughing so hard we could almost see his esophagus. I shooed him away with the umbrella and he stepped in a puddle, stomping his feet to splash us. The boys' shirts were splattered with mud. Fredo ripped the umbrella away from me with both hands and stabbed it into the tip of the boy's foot. Shots had to be fired into the air to disperse the mob that began to form. They wanted to lynch us. The principal made me promise that we would never come back. Not ever.

Face Imitates Form

When I brought up operating on the boys, Doctor Umpiérrez, a young surgeon at Fulgencio López Hospital, recommended trimming them down into one. At the risk of losing both.

"It's simple. We cannot consider ManFredo two subjects just because he has two heads. Legally he is one identity. His fingerprints, his genitals, and his heart are only one. You must decide which brain is less valuable."

"Relative to what?" asked the Colonel.

"To whatever your criteria may be. I'd be inclined toward ecumenical values: strength, bravery, aggression," Umpiérrez offered.

Domingo proposed we keep Fredo, who had more potential. Man cried all night. I consoled him and told him that we'd settle it with the impartiality of chance. But the next day, he'd prepared some words that he read courageously at breakfast:

"I'm sacrificing myself for the family. My life is over anyway. I suffer social segregation, Mother's repulsed look, Father's distance, and my brother's contempt. May my death serve a purpose, because my life does not."

We thanked him for his generosity and that night we all went out to a French restaurant.

Fredo's attitude made me suspicious. He made a toast with an immense smile. He couldn't hide how happy his brother's disappearance made him. He was exultant. I had to kick him under the table. Unfortunately it was Man who felt the pain.

"What's wrong, Mother?"

"Nothing, a cramp, I'm sorry."

The Colonel was oblivious. Or didn't care.

"The body and the name won't change, right? It's all the same to me. One less opinion," Domingo concluded.

Fucking masculine practicality. I had doubts on the way to the hospital. But later I said to myself: Let the best one win.

Operation Massacre

After hours of uncertainty, Umpiérrez appeared with a leaden expression. The operation hadn't come out as hoped.

"When we compressed the Siamese into one, something unexpected occurred," the doctor confessed. "The gray matter is highly compromised. One appendage can be operated on, but the ideas are difficult to locate. Who controls what? How do you excise a thought? Who dreamed what, where do memories reside? We found external ideas too, and didn't know whether to save them all or do a massive purge. One of the boys was a good reader. We found entire paragraphs of Ovid's *Metamorphosis*. You have to understand, the brain as an object is one thing and knowledge something else entirely. In this case, there's the added complexity of the double. We might have gone too far, but by saving some useless yet deeply rooted memories, we lost entire chapters."

"But the operation came out okay?" I said, exhausted.

"Yes. But I must warn you, ManFredo has three hemispheres now. Two left and one right. Or maybe two right and one left. Time will tell, based on the nature of his actions. It's possible he'll be interested in the arts or in the opposite—in decency. We'll have to wait and see."

"What?" said the Colonel, stunned.

"The incomplete piece of brain is a parasite, living off the other. Don't ask me which is which. They won't even know. The one controlling the mouth will change. Up close, you'll be able to tell them apart. Even by their breath. But at a distance, they'll look like one giant head."

"What a travesty."

"With a good hat he'll be set. At least he won't attract as much attention as before."

"So, Man is still alive?" I said.

"In effect. Inside his brother's brain. Or the other way around."

"Oh, I'm so glad. I don't feel quite so guilty."

"They look like three tangerine slices," Yedra said when we got home.

Nobody laughed.

Sitting from Four to Five

It's been several weeks since they killed me. I'm assuming. It's hard for me to keep track of time. Without me, the family routines have changed. Every so often, they go visit Buda.

Yedra dresses the boys in striped shirts and bow ties. Like when they were little.

My sister is wrinkled, but in good health. She's the only connection to my family left. She has no children and never married. She and the Colonel never got along, but since my death, they've constructed a parody. They drink tea and flip through the family album, or photographs from my old shows. My death gives them life.

When Man wants to sit, Fredo won't let him. So the Colonel proposes a compromise: sitting from four to five, standing from five to six. In the silent pauses, they bicker.

Buda detests Fredo and when he leaves, she promises never to see him again. But it's a promise she can't keep. She knows next Thursday it'll be the same. And on like that until the last minute. Because despite everything, it does her good to spend time with Man, to look him deep in the eyes, where the dead woman hides. She sees me in his gray irises. Our eyes meet without anybody knowing it. Buda tolerates the whims of the one, so she can see me in the other.

I was mother to a horrible synthesis. I see them now, snacking in my sister's house and thank science for its advances. You can barely tell.

When they finish snacking, they say goodbye to Buda and I follow them. The return home, along wet or dry sidewalks, looking like the tail end of a military parade, where the cadets have lost precision and integrity. Their boots are fuller and their feet fatter, softened by sweat.

Furtive glances follow ManFredo and the Colonel to the door of the house.

Lana waits for Domingo in the little room, scantily clad, and they bolt the door. I watch them have a drink or make love in silence. She tells him she cries for me. She's a liar. He just strokes her hair like a boy in love.

How can you love a foam-rubber imposter?

Buda and I

My sister was always an unknown quantity. In contrast to my adventurous character, she was withdrawn. Just talking in front of her embarrassed me sometimes. She knew my excesses.

I think that, for her, I was always a subject of anthropological interest. I never understood what she wanted. She never asked for anything.

"Tell me about yourself," I'd say to her.

"Nothing to say. Life's not offering much in the way of novelty."

"It's reciprocal."

"You think?"

"Yes. It depends on you. Give it some headlines."

"I do things, but nothing comes of it. My fate is so moderate. And that's how I like it. Abundance upsets me."

We maintained an extended silence to keep from arguing. I would have liked to get her worked up, even against her will. I never got up the nerve.

Now, I visit her late at night. Invariably she's awake, sitting up in bed. Eyes defeated by the awareness of a perennial insomnia. Maybe she senses me. I don't know.

I suppose we'll always be side by side: two parallel lines.

Pandora, Sad-Song Music Box

A month before my patriotic execution, during the general end-of-month cleaning, something dramatic happened.

I had established a monthly tournament of chores and obligations with soap and scrub brush that the family participated in without complaint. I swapped out traditional customs for a life of hygiene with no quarter given to leisure or indifference.

The day began at six in the morning with an aggressive blow of my whistle. Ten minutes later, everyone was assembled around the little table by the laundry room, where I passed out a sheet with assignments, written out in excessive detail. I inspected the results with a martial gaze, honoring the winner with a cloth medal.

It's not hard to imagine why ManFredo couldn't stand me. He would have preferred to sleep in, to be free. To enjoy the privilege of youth. Man, for his part, had long ago resigned himself to never receiving any affection. But he didn't blame me, he blamed his appearance, his severed deformity. Who can love a child like that, he repeated to the silence. That's why the cloth medals upset him. The Colonel went to the Restó Militaire for the duration of the competition. He sipped an anisette by the window, and didn't speak to anyone.

That morning, I decided to clean the darkroom. Moving some boxes that were partially hidden in the back of the room, I stumbled across a disturbing trove of treasures. A photograph of me, in my underwear. Little love letters. Press clippings with erect nipples. Blood-red garters. The Colonel's notes. And photographs of Lana, superimposed. Domingo hadn't held anything back. He'd even photographed the boys in aberrant positions, with her riding them. Nauseous *découpage*, teeming with life. Fredo's leering half smile, his flexed muscles.

But worst of all was finding that pair of legs dangling from a hanger. Exquisite extremities sculpted out of some flexible material. In boxes there were twenty-five pairs of size-six shoes for those fake feet. There was foam-rubber stuffing, motors removed from electronic devices, and a couple half-finished torsos.

I sat down in front of that glimpse of the future. I wanted to hurl it all against the wall, to make a scene. But it was already too late. Yedra met my eyes, her lips curling in a smile.

Everyone knew but me.

The Colonel's Notes

1. Windup Lana

She's coming along. She doesn't look like a hunk of wood anymore. The inverted clock that runs her gives her a certain air of mystery. She's like a memory made material. Her face, unfathomable.

Looking at her, I feel complete.

For her debut, I'll call everyone into the dining room (everyone but Aurora). At my signal, Yedra will turn off the light and Lana will do her free-rhythm dance.

. . .

I took advantage of my wife's absence to put on the first show. ManFredo sat in the beige armchair. A curtain opened and Lana began to dance. It was a powerful synthesis of woman and sounding box. Multiple metaphysical truths pressed together in her body, beginning with the origin of being, the abstraction of ideas, and the power of music. Her spirit squeals, animated by her mechanical movement.

She knows how to open and close her mouth, wordlessly. No footstep is free of chance, her axis shifts and surprises. Facedown, or poised on one leg, her bodyweight coincides with an unpredictable syllabication.

ManFredo was captivated by her physical prowess. For a moment he forgot himself. Contemplating the empty woman frees us.

I let myself get swept up in longing for transcendence. To behold Lana is to glimpse a form of immortality. It simultaneously elevates and devastates.

But the show's number ended with a snap. No applause. The alarm suddenly went off and the windup mechanism spun out of control. I had to withdraw her right away.

She'll be under observation for a week.

2. Pedal Lana

I'm excited about this new prototype. It's been hours since I ingested any liquids. The darkroom has become my refuge. This lunacy my salvation. Aurora continues her routine of degradations and complaints. She says they love her more at the committee than at home. For once she's right.

· · ·

Emulating the distance shutter, I've inserted a cable into Lana that connects to Yedra's sewing machine. When I push the pedals, she turns on. And yet, the limitation of the cord is discouraging. And

I don't want to have to ask anything of my cousin. Something will go wrong.

Before modifying her, I took a photo with Lana. I picked up an aquamarine backdrop and a sky-blue cravat at Mercado de Pulgas. We looked like lovers in a lukewarm fishbowl. I kissed her nipples. Then I called ManFredo. He posed like a pro.

3. Nine-Volt Lana

In addition to modifying her structure (I inserted Bakelite joints in her elbows, knees, neck, and ankles), I've eliminated the loofa and craft paper. It got swollen in the rain. I've substituted a synthetic sponge: so even if she gets wet, she doesn't get bloated. She just gets heavier. I redid some lacquer details and changed her eyes. I got some glass eyes from the optician, very similar to those of the original. Grayish-blue.

• • •

The battery gives her two hours of utility. While Aurora sleeps, we stare into each other's eyes. I took some photos by the flagpole. When I wasn't paying attention, Yedra grabbed her before I could react. She dragged her to the little room. Along the way, their eyes met. Yedra pulled the battery from her thorax and Lana ceased to be. She dropped her by the workbench and shut the door. I slapped her without thinking. Slapped Yedra. I ran to my creation, kissed her while reinserting her battery. I felt the shudder of her coming back to life.

4. Solar Lana

Fortunately, Aurora was gone all day at the hospital. They're planning a fundraiser. The important thing is that her absence gives me time to be happy.

The episode with Yedra inspired me to install a double battery in Lana. But then I decided to radically alter her system. I've created a dress out of photovoltaic material. A polypropylene blend—resistant to sunlight, oxidation, and electrolysis—that maintains its elasticity even under adverse climatic conditions.

During daylight hours, I charge her by the window. Sometimes we go out and take a little stroll together in the courtyard. These outings inspired me to teach her to sing "You Belong to My Heart," as a duet.

Last night, we were whispering the refrain when Yedra appeared. But before she could do anything, I took her into the kitchen and bolted the door. To calm her and make her understand. I don't want her to touch my Lana. I forbid it. She looks at me as if I were a madman, but it doesn't matter. Morality is a joke. It's a symptom of mediocrity.

5. Lana Carne

(still formless)

Latin Disorder

I waited for Yedra beside the discovered legs. I was nervous. She leaned against the door. Our eyes met. With a look she indicated the darkroom's little curtain. I went in and turned on the light. The space was stained red as if it were reading my thoughts. She was in one corner. Photovoltaic Lana, in repose. I bent down to get a better look. She was smiling. The little whore was smiling like a demented angel.

The Colonel had moved on to action. His childish creation made me weep, overcome with emotion. How he loved her. I'd been distracted with the committee, with Horacio, while he'd been fabricating his little paradise. A graceless Eden that awaited him among the acid solutions in the warmth of his darkroom.

I picked her up in my arms, like somebody rescuing a baby from a fire. I carried her out to the courtyard. Yedra followed me. The ManFredos stopped arguing and lowered the blinds.

The midday sun beat furiously down. I left her on the ground by the flag and ran to find the magnifying glass. There, at her pathetic heart I aimed the glass. At first a tiny wisp of smoke, then a click. I watched her burn. Writhing in fear. She lit up like a magic lantern. Her stomach flared. She folded in at her fake navel. I watched her become fully engulfed in flame.

That's when Domingo got home. He didn't look at me. He stood motionless in front of that mound of wretchedness. He buried her remains in the courtyard, under the jasmine. And never said another word to me.

I thought he'd give up then, but he's a soldier. A professional of guerrilla warfare. When I learned he was building another Lana, I felt nothing but shame. I let him do it.

There was nothing left between us. Domingo—literally—sawed our marital bed in half. After that, we slept in our own beds.

Horacio Tabardi, Recoil

The accountant was always a man of unmanageable curls. Despite the hair gel. He always looked freshly showered, but never fresh. I hadn't seen him since before my wedding. But loneliness is a wily beast and one day, coming home from the committee, it put him in my path.

I recognized him right away. He was wearing an overcoat that looked like a crumpled paper bag. Brown and wrinkled. Slit in the back. He kicked the immense jacket along as he walked. Accountants often fall victim to their own overcoats.

He gave me such a surprising look that it dawned on me how dull my life had become.

"You're beautiful," he said, and I felt washed-up, hideous.

Before long, I started taking better care of myself. Domesticity and the physical and moral deformity I was mired in had tarnished my glow. I bought some new dresses and scarves, fixed my hair. I even started wearing lipstick when I went out.

Horacio and I began an affair. We were drawn to each other in a serendipitous manner. Turning a corner, Horacio. Leaving the committee, again.

One afternoon, I bared my thighs at a little hotel downtown

and there he was again. Kissing my zones like he owned them.

How we wound up there, I really can't say. But it was more intense than the first time. It began with a coffee, an innocent stroll. Walks down well-worn avenues. We even coincided in our stride. Left / right / left. Then we moved on to more vigorous activities.

One day I discovered that he was writing me little notes, and leaving them in my jacket pocket. *If I tremble it's because of you.* A kind of convulsion shot through my whole body and doubled me over. *Your love bursts in my marrow.*

Sometimes, one of his eyes would shoot back without warning. Or his head. As if he'd stuck his fingers in the holes of a socket. And I don't mean me. Whenever one or all of his curls popped up, I laughed. His fits were funny, like he was controlled by a puppet master with tangled strings. He was seized by waves of electricity and, whether I was on top or not, his shaking infected me. Like riding an electric bull. I dug my heels in and arched back and forward. Dying of vertigo. Pleasure looks a lot like mental illness.

In this love, everything was body. Mounting the bull, riding the sweet beast, writhing. I lost all the weight I'd put on during my marriage. Cohabitation nurtures emptiness, a void you fill by eating. Betrayal makes you thin.

When I came home, Domingo didn't notice me, distracted with his latest Lana. But I felt my indiscretion lapping at every tile. *Bite me and I'll bite back.* The world smelled of Horacio. In other words, of hair gel. The boys, the bed, the bathroom, the table, the surgeon, my tongue. The persistence of his smell disturbed me. The messages in my pocket. *You, my tamer. Bending gypsy, thieving temptress. Thinking of you, that's all I do.*

He spun them out like a poet. And there's nothing more dangerous than a man who manipulates lines and verses with delight.

The image of him naked pursues me everywhere. I thought I saw us tangled together, more than once. His strong and swarthy buttocks pumped a sharp cadence. He hammered my body in three times and then more, rough pounding. He was the nail and I, his purpose. Pierced and polished wood. When we finished, I washed and said to myself: This will pass. You'll forget him. But no. My desire for him was an ache without cure.

Our last afternoon, we'd gone to the zoo and he decided to show me a picture of his wife. I was aware of her existence, but seeing her there disappointed me. A fat little woman with a warm predisposition smiled up at me, with the unsettling expression of a failing schoolgirl. Suddenly, the scope of what I was encouraging dawned on me. Harming that poor woman gave me no satisfaction. And it also aroused a competitive feeling in me and my rival was next to nothing.

How to escape an unfamiliar garden without damaging the flora. Mine was the worst possible strategy. Trampling.

"There's no room for you in my life," I said after a moment, as if it were a deliberate decision and not the product of an uncomfortable thought. "We're impossible, you and I. Don't come for me, there's nothing you can do."

It took him a while to react. There was an elephant nearby. I remember the putrid stench of its defecations. Its force was enough to cut through Horacio's hair gel, to reduce it to an irrelevant nothing.

Taking advantage of his hesitation, I quickly abandoned the premises. I deprived him of explanations and context. I just walked purposefully to the main gate, my nostrils flaring. My heart heavy. Regrettably, I couldn't resist the temptation to look back.

Head bent, staring at his knees, his body began to shake. A cocktail of curls seized control of him. Visitors stopped to stare. An old man went to help him. I picked up my pace, jogging. A mortal fear gripped my face. Let her take care of him, the woman from the photo. Fucking pathetic couple.

I finally made it home and, in my pocket with my keys, I discovered a last little note. *I'm waiting for you there.*

The imprecision made me laugh. I threw it away, trying to forget what happened.

Over the next two months, I thought I saw him a thousand times. But it was never him. Just desire messing with my head. Every brown overcoat was a potential Horacio. That battalion of villains pursued me even in dreams. An army of accountants, naked under brown folds.

It wasn't love. I was tainted. Out of focus. I thought he would come for me, but no.

One morning, I saw his picture in the paper. I recognized him by his hair.

ACCOUNTANT JUMPS OFF THIRD-STORY BALCONY.

Those Left Behind

Days without me. It no longer unsettles me. I'm getting used to being dead. The Colonel is always with Lana. Seeing me dead, he gave himself to that lifeless other. Domingo gets pleasure from what doesn't exist. Reality moves too fast.

Yedra is very upset with him.

"After everything I did!" she repeats a few centimeters from the door.

I think she's referring to me. To my death. Maybe she's the culprit. But I don't feel resentment. She's the only one who thinks of me. You have to value someone to kill them. I make myself her accomplice. I almost understand her. The others have forgotten me.

If Horacio were alive, I'd visit him from time to time. I wouldn't care about his wife anymore. Death gives another perspective. I'd sit with them at breakfast time, and the three of us would sleep together on winter nights. I'd fix myself to the inside of his overcoat.

I failed to give that man precise dimension. My priorities were mistaken.

I think again about the elephant, the only vestige of our love.

Sad monster, huge effigy of love. Trapped inside its foul enclosure. Not even a memory of its free past. Despite the ears, the beast doesn't hear. Or plays dumb.

Hours lost thinking of the pachyderm as a metaphor for immobility. If thought is action, the premise is not confirmed. I want to touch ideas. To make a body anew. To suck the skin or lips of someone sweet.

All I have are words, which is to say, not a trace.

Two of Them, Miserable Action

When the others dream, Man's eyes remain open. Riven with ideas he can't direct. Fredo's violent snoring takes up too much space and the only way to fight back is to shut himself in the den of his own hemisphere. He spends long hours thinking phrases of protest before falling asleep. Sometimes, insomnia keeps him captive until the first bird of morning. Night sets him free.

Fredo wakes unexpectedly.

"If I look at her, I'll drool on her."

"Who're you talking about?"

"Silvia. She wrote down *monster* in her notebook. It was me. You."

"We."

Fredo dreams of appearing in the psychologist's nocturnal borderlands, his strength illuminated.

"I want to have sex. I'm planning how."

"Not with me."

"We're in it together."

But it's not true. Some things escape them. Both of them. The night before, while Fredo slept, Man played with himself. It was the only possible time. It was strange. At times he didn't know who felt the pleasure. Where he begins, where his person ends. Borders blur. Lines run together. Just as he thinks the body is his, Fredo takes over. Moving extremities he thought under his control. The war is endless. Insufficient space for all that mind. It's impossible to come. Man gets distracted observing the phenomenon and the body becomes terrifying.

Fredo mistreats him. Sometimes it's like he hates him. Every morning he wakes up with a face of disgust, sick of his side of things.

The Colonel does what he can, which isn't much. He talks to Fredo, to get him to be more thoughtful. Man feigns disinterest, but listens in. It's impossible not to participate in the misery. Fredo laughs and considers putting Man to sleep, but he's afraid the effects of a sedative would bifurcate and make him sleepy. Sometimes he feels like there's a rock tied to his neck. It's his mirror, and it drags him down.

Man's mind is full of complaints like this:

Fredo thinks he can confuse me. He told me to shut my eyes. He bought me a key ring. What would I do with a key ring? We're left-handed and he controls the left hand. I guess it's a diabolical way of mocking me. Besides, I don't like to go out.

The only thing he respects is my writing time. I hope that doesn't change. I feel bound to a sick creature. He inspects me, controls me, deprives me of solitude—the one good thing. It should be a legitimate right for everyone.

Rising

One of the few things I appreciate about my present state is the freedom. Death has no limits. I share the thoughts of any mind. Ideas aren't restricted to the head's diameter, they're an amorphous blotch, imprecise.

Sometimes you believe you've understood something on your own just because it coincided in space with another thought. Then you assume you came up with it. That you imagined something. But the world is already invented. The point of view is all that changes.

Mental disturbances take shape before me like words written on a foggy mirror. I see liquid figures and submerge myself in them.

I read minds lazily, inconclusive states, meaningless fragments, foul or vacuous little clouds, underdeveloped opinions, unnoticed even by the one responsible for expressing them, opinions that fall apart before coming together. Abortions of thought.

Other times, less often, I'm drawn to their level of precision. Like beef consommé. Ideas or hysterical contortions, now you see it, now you don't. There are empty heads too. Mental breakdowns that remain corralled.

My death is incomplete. Or my life. I don't understand how everyone else dies without some part of them being left behind.

Man's Brain, Defense

13:30

Father is pleased with his newest Lana. Yedra lost it when she went into the workshop and Lana fell to the floor. Father cried in the beginning and Yedra in the end. An ugly day for everyone.

Later he was able to get the girl to open and close her mouth, without the previous complications. He's teaching her to talk. Or that's what he thinks. When he left the room, I asked Fredo to come touch her curls with me. They're real and smell of lavender. But he said something shocking about rubbing himself against the subject. That's what he called her. Sexual subject. He says he wants to refine his style, practice positions, concoct scenarios. Apparently he's tired of Yedra.

19:45

Fredo told the psychologist that bothering him makes me happy. That my lofty moral sensibility is a hindrance, that I'm like Pinocchio's cricket, all day naysaying. That he feels hemmed in by the double consciousness (he didn't put it like that): his and mine, which is galling because it never lets up. He also said that he wants "to fuck the mannequin." Silvia laughed and I tried to get up, to abandon the divan. Fredo didn't even move, he held fast, and we wound up on the floor. She helped us up and I inadvertently brushed against her breast. Her body smells like wheat. Then she suggested expanding the representative or symbolic significance of Father's creation. She says that for Fredo she could be a geisha and, for me, a substitute for the maternal love I never had. Sometimes psychologists go too far. According to her, identifying Lana with Mother would amount to giving her a new significance.

I was seized by a coughing fit when I heard that ludicrous hypothesis. We choked. Silvia grabbed my arms to try to help and almost fell on top of us. Then I distinctly felt Fredo's sudden erection. A horrible feeling. I don't want to witness his private life.

I struggled and managed to get us upright. I refuse to participate in acts of dubious morality. Again.

22:13

When we got home, Father was watching TV with Lana. They looked like a normal married couple. If it weren't for the fact that the wife was a piece of furniture. Or maybe that was why.

When I got closer, I saw that Father was aroused. He wasn't even watching the show. He'd slipped a hand under her dress.

This upset me because I'd resolved to resist feeling melancholy. Fredo got angry, tried to touch her, and ripped off one of her arms. Father almost got the gun.

Next time I see her in the living room, I'll kill her, Fredo said. You are not allowed near me, or her, Father answered. Don't talk to me like a child, Fredo shot back. Give me the arm, Father demanded. Enough, I shouted. And my voice broke.

Father retreated without the arm. His face got so red it was frightening. I thought he was going to explode. I wanted to run away, not to witness something like that. So sad and so ridiculous. Fredo threw the arm on the floor. He was furious. On one of Lana's fingers, Mother's amethyst.

Father doesn't want to forget her. Or at least that's what he'd said. But the subject hasn't come up again. Besides she looks like someone else. Like Father's great love, that's what Yedra said. I stole the ring without anybody noticing.

00:49

When Fredo fell asleep, I kept thinking. I still had the amethyst. I was cold and felt someone touch my shoulder. It was Father. He gestured for me to stay quiet. He was hiding something. When he was sure that Fredo was sleeping, he brought her out in front of me.

"She wants to say something," Father said.

"Who?" I whispered.

"Her."

"No way."

"Yes, she says a few words."

"Show me."

The strange woman opened her lips.

"I'm Lana. I want you to play with me."

I didn't respond. Father gestured but couldn't soothe me. I looked them in the eyes, her first. A tear, a bubble of sadness slid down her cheek, and I looked away. Then they left. Her face was familiar. And I don't mean Mother. I'm talking about death.

Oneiric Fredo, Attack of Passion

It happened again. If I close my eyes I'm in the park. Hair slicked back like a tango singer. Alone, beautiful. Between the flaming foliage and the fierce gazes of the schoolgirls who watch me. I dance like a faun in their eyes.

Under an ash tree, I present my profile, silhouetted by a red and primitive sun that dips below the horizon. The branches are dark lips whispering of longing.

Suddenly, a strange wind blows and the park is swept away and I'm in my bedroom. Breathing black breath. A door opens suddenly. Someone shoots me in the chest. A sharp and feverish pain seizes my life. The weak part of me collapses and I try to run, but I'm on the floor.

The group of hungry schoolgirls emerge from the closet, take hold of the bullet, and pull with all of their might to remove it from my body. That bright object grows in their hands, morphing into a penis, a person. A beautiful newborn.

Man emerges from the casing. The schoolgirls coo at him, come to his rescue, wiping him clean with their short skirts. He's raised into that new sky, while I'm left on the floor, with an open wound. Bleeding in silence. Blinded by the inferno.

To the physical challenges you must add the stupid morality of the schoolgirls of my dreams. Let's cradle the amorphous thing, the sad monster. I pervert the game: looking like this, I can't be decent.

The Suppositions of Yedra

I think the *señora* is alive. I sense her. It's not that I smell her perfume. It's not that I hear her breathing. It's not that. I hear her heartbeat. If I touch the walls, I feel her pulse. The house still throbs with her. If she's dead, she's taking a while to depart.

When the boys come to my bed, I see her blinking in the door. So I let myself want it, to take revenge. Now she has to witness the sordidness. Your turn, *Señora*. And I kiss the boys, make them mine.

On the way to the dining room, I hear her high heels. The hardwood floor echoes differently with the frustrated footsteps of a dead woman. And I'll follow her wherever she leads. She never liked inventions. Never appreciated Domingo's wild imagination. Poor thing, if she knew the truth, she'd die for real.

When the Colonel goes to bed, I'll go to his room, make things clear. The new Lana sleeps alone. Watch yourself, whore.

Her Red Room, a Show

A few days before my death, the therapist proposed that Fredo pay to have sex outside the home, but the Colonel and I said no. He was worried ManFredo wouldn't be allowed in any of the brothels. That the girls would laugh or freak out at the size of his head.

In my case it was pure moral scruple. The pleasure of others seemed vile to me. And the fact that there were two of them. The orgy never appealed to me. Too depraved.

At therapy, they laid out the boys' hormonal future.

"I can't wait any longer," Fredo blubbered in the office, as a cold image sank into his pores.

"But I don't want to," Man insisted decisively.

"Well, we can't deprive Fredo of his desire. Think of a way to confront your individual sexualities, without upsetting the other," Silvia suggested.

She asks the impossible. But she dresses like a professional, so everyone just accepts it. She's tired of other peoples' problems. She wants to get away but doesn't know how. I'm an ear, she tells herself. A hole everyone dumps their filth into. But from the eardrum right to amnesia.

Sometimes she gets her patients mixed up. All personal fables end up resembling each other. She loves me, she loves me not. They fucked me up. Simple phrases embodied in every mouth. Be patient, Heine tells herself, feeling the movement of her breathing.

"You know what you have to do. The rest is superfluous," she says, and they nod in agreement.

According to Fredo's plan, at four thirty the next day a specialist would pay them a visit. Yedra asks for the afternoon off. She doesn't want to hear the lust, the moans. They found the girl in the paper, striking an excessively vulgar pose.

"If it's the one in the picture, I'll have to bleach the sheets," Yedra said before leaving.

I went to the committee in a state of confusion, but then forgot the whole thing. The *hipertensas* operated on instant oblivion. I think that's what we were there for. Charity begins with oneself. You give, and receive indifference. You set aside your own needs, as if trading one misfortune for another. Someone else suffers so something different happens to us, the omission of the self always comes from outside.

Man was nervous. Now that I'm dead, I can access the facts. He recorded the episode in his diary.

Man's Personal Diary
(Don't Read)

10:00

I asked Fredo that they blindfold us:

"I don't want to watch you getting off."

"And me, how will I see her?"

The girl's arrival is set for seven thirty. Yedra retired after wash-ing the midday dishes. The Colonel shut himself in his little room. Mother went to take her blood pressure to pressure us. She says we're going to break her heart.

"You're trembling," Fredo mocked. "When the girl gets here, don't say anything. I think, after this experience, I'll be a better person."

"We'll see."

I decide to put a patch over my left eye to hide my shame, though only partially.

20:04

The girl is ringing the bell. We spy on her without her knowing.

She's young and looks nothing like the girl in the photo. She seems inexperienced. She applies thick, plum-colored rouge on the doorstep. She's a cripple.

Fredo puts on schmaltzy music to welcome her and spritzes himself with excess cologne. I turn off the lights and approach her in the dark, a blind eye and a quaking soul. Then, everything happens at a diabolical speed.

"Good evening."

"It's so dark."

"For the nerves."

"Who said that?"

"My brother."

"Where is he?"

"What are you, a reporter?"

"It'll cost more. It's a different price for two."

"I don't want anything."

"Shut up, Man."

"Leave him be, poor thing. Is he a *voyeur*?"

"No, Argentine."

"Do you have an aspirin? I've got a headache."

"No."

"I have some."

"Why are you hiding? You afraid of me?"

"Not of you, I'm afraid of being disgusted seeing him with you."

"And so why do you stay?"

"Take off your clothes."

"It's cold."

"Turn on the furnace, Fredo."

"Don't tell me what to do!"

"What's his name? The other guy."

"Man. And you?"

"Norma."

"That's funny. I am part of your name."

"How do you mean?"

"Nor Ma. I am in there, but disassembled."

"Show me something, babe. You're not here to talk."

"Everything okay?"

"Yes, Father. Will you go away? I can hear you breathing through the door."

"There's Fernet in the cupboard."

"Bye, Father."

"Man?"

"Yes, Father."

"Have a little drink."

"No, I don't like it."

"To get in the mood."

"Got it."

"Can you go away, Father? And you, what're you doing?"

"I wanted to kiss her."

"I turn my back for a minute and you go ahead without me?"

"It was her. She's sweet."

"Come here."

"Oh!"

"On your knees."

"Don't talk to her like that."

"It's fine, I'm used to it."

"Kneel, please. And then lean forward, facedown."

I feel a tightness in my chest.

"This isn't going well, pass me the receiver."

"It's a different price with objects."

"I'm talking about the phone."

"Ah."

"What was it?"

"996-2532."

"Doctor?"

"Yes, who is this?"

"It's Fredo."

"How are you?"

"I'm here, with a whore."

"Norma."

"Shut up."

"And is Man okay?"

"Perfect. Turns out it doesn't work for me."

"What do you mean?"

"Mine doesn't work, Man's does, and he didn't even do anything."

"But if it's the same . . . Hang on, let me talk to him."

"Hello, Silvia."

"What happened?"

"Norma is here for him and I was the one who got aroused. Against my will."

"You didn't like it?"

"It's the situation."

"Man, why don't you let yourself enjoy the moment?"

"Because Fredo is here."

"He'll always be there."

"Let me talk to Silvia."

"Fredo wants to tell you something."

"Hang on . . ."

"Doctor, what do I do?"

"Everything okay?"

"Father, I'm on the phone."

"How are things, Colonel?"

"Ah, excuse me, Doctor. I didn't know you were on the phone."

"Father, hang up."

"Sorry."

"No problem."

"Silvia, what do I do?"

"Maybe the object of desire doesn't live up to your expectations."

"But then why does it work for Man?"

"Calm down. We'll analyze it during session on Monday."

"Monday?"

"Relax now and enjoy yourselves even if it's not what you'd imagined. Being there, for now, is enough. Let me talk to Man for a second."

"She wants to talk to you."

"Man?"

"Yes."

"You had an erection!"

"Settle down, Doctor."

"How do you feel?"

"Confused."

"He came, Silvia! He got everything and I got nothing."

"Tell your brother to calm down."

"He's really upset."

"I can't talk now, I have a patient. See you Monday."

"Okay, but I don't know if . . ."

"What'd she say?"

"She hung up."

"Bitch."

"I have to go. Who's going to pay me?"

When she turns on the light, Norma discovers that we're only one person.

"What're you, a ventriloquist?"

But nobody answers her. Fredo and I argue. He refuses to pay for a service he hasn't used. I decide to pay and I feel an unexpected sense of superiority.

20:47

Norma gives us her card and leaves with a scowl. On her way out, Father intercepts her. I think they go somewhere together. I hope I'm wrong. I see them moving in the direction of the little darkroom and already I know. Father gets off on the anomalous. The girl is very unstable on her left leg. And it sounds hollow, even.

22

Tomorrow is the boys' birthday. Man suggests they stay home and have a healthy meal. He knows what awaits them out there. Stares, snickers, whispers, heckles, people's banal attempts to pretend they didn't notice. Bearing the cross of the freak-show phenomenon.

But Fredo and the Colonel want to go out, need to cross the threshold of isolation and open themselves up to the world.

Yedra will iron their sky-blue shirt and the Colonel will give each of them a gift. They'll go to the Restó Militaire, a family restaurant with Napoleonic airs full of old retirees from the armed forces.

Man will suffer, Fredo will be fine. The Colonel hasn't felt anything for a long time. He suggests that Lana come along. But on that point the boys are in agreement.

"No," they say in unison.

Man wanted to stay home. The dread of knowing and being alone is impossible. He dreams of it and wakes up in tears, when he sees that no. Man rushes to make impressions in the inviolable corner of his head. He knows Fredo captures the most superficial thoughts the moment he thinks them. Reading his ideas like someone scanning the headlines of a newspaper. There's nothing

Man can do but separate his feelings into a winding and inaccessible seam.

They'll call for a car. Always the same one. They don't want an unprepared driver. It happened once. He drove them all over the neighborhood honking the horn and pointing at the *deformes*. That's what he called them. Fredo grabbed him from behind, and the Colonel yanked the handbrake. They almost choked him.

At the restaurant they'll order rabbit. Except for Man, who's a vegetarian and will order a salad. Fredo will impatiently devour half a rabbit, narcotizing his palate with a potent Merlot—the family's preferred varietal.

Man knows what comes next. When Fredo drinks too much, they go to Yedra's room. At first she resists, but in the end lets it happen.

So Man drinks a lot of water, to counteract the alcohol in the body of his double. He wants to avoid the old crone. But the water runs down their shared throat and trickles into Man's world, missing Fredo, who remains drunk and exultant.

After pudding, after coffee and liquor, after multiple trips to the bathroom, the three of them will make their way home.

Fredo's songs burst from his throat like malevolent arrows. They deafen Man and irritate the Colonel. But that doesn't stop him. A tuneless provocateur.

When they get home, the only thing on Fredo's mind is entering Yedra's body. After fooling around with auntie, they'll go back to their room.

Man will want to shower and Fredo will say yes. The Colonel has installed a double shower system with mobile arms that allows them to set different temperatures. Man washes with scalding water. Fredo does not.

Under a double stream, hot or cold, Fredo lets loose a fresh diatribe.

"Father spoke with Silvia this morning and they agree. I should satisfy my desire."

"Again?"

"I also told him what you said, about how you don't want to be human."

"I didn't say that."

"You said it. Verbatim."

"I said that I don't feel human, which is very different."

"Same thing. Father proposed we take photos with the little whore."

"Pass."

"He said he'd pay us."

"Father? I don't want to."

"It's already a done deal. We're going to use some of his real medals. Who knows where we'll put them."

I see the Colonel going to Lana. And I stay in the living room, not moving. I watch the moon drop out of sight and an immense loneliness rises to replace it. My loneliness hangs in the sky and doesn't shine. It's a black stone.

Life Surrenders

Domingo presented his machine again today. After dinner. He wanted to publicly validate his advances.

She's got on one of my old dresses. It's too big. She looks like a past version of me, equally skinny and despicable.

The family gathers with skepticism in the living room.

"Good evening. Lana is a little clumsy with language, don't respond to her. We have figured out how to move our eyes more quickly thanks to a double spatula screw that lets us blink more gracefully," the Colonel explains, gesticulating absurdly.

"Who?"

"Her."

"Don't use the plural," Fredo commands. "You sound like a civil servant or a guy selling feather dusters."

"You don't have to be rude," Man intervenes.

"Thanks, Son. Let's proceed. If she tries hard, Lana can also smile in an almost human way."

"But she doesn't know what it is to smile?" jabs Yedra, surprisingly sharp.

"She knows. Let's see, Lana. Smile."

Lana smiles without conviction.

"She might be able to simulate a space between jawbones. But without a soul you can't smile," Yedra points out, subtle and suddenly poetic.

"Quiet, please. Don't upset her," the Colonel demands, pursing his mustache ever so slightly.

Lana whispers in the inventor's ear and touches her chest, like an offended actress. I can't stay. I'd rather wait outside, listen to their heads without the filter of their bodies.

I have to admit that in recent days I've begun to feel a vague revulsion. The odors and material attitudes of my family nauseate me and clearly I can't purge, no matter how the disgust swells and gags me. I feel flooded with horror, an unfathomable desolation.

I want to die. I beg for my end.

Man

I think Father is worse than we thought. When his creature was talking, I watched him. A horrible glow seized his eyes. It was pride. And more than the object, seeing that delusion of grandeur filled me with dread. It's not just Fredo anymore, now I hate the whole family. Only Yedra demonstrated any common sense, but she was harshly reprimanded. I hope she doesn't leave.

After seeing Lana's half-naked body, I've been thinking again about suicide. But it's unclear what would happen to Fredo if I die. I guess they can't excise me from his side. And I don't want him to end up carrying my coffin. That's why I've not yet gotten up the nerve to discuss my disappearance with Silvia. I'm afraid I'll just provoke cynical laughter from everyone.

Fredo

The madwoman looked at me. And I can't forget that precarious glance. There was a spark between us. There were times, taking a step with her shoddy foot, I saw her eyes meet my lips. An ardent lover is hidden there. Under the rudimentary surface trembles an unknown form of desire in a pure state. Nobody could conceal it, reduce it. It's Father's great achievement.

How can I be with her in my own right? I won't settle for a substitute.

Yedra

Today I clearly felt the dead woman's presence. She must be shocked. The new Lana's poses coincide exactly with the stills from the movie we watched. They look identical. Domingo programmed her in image and semblance.

I think Aurora suffers, even in death. Her absence has served nothing. I'm a fanatic of her presence.

Domingo

How odd. Lana Carne's lack of humanity upsets the family. Under the dress and the accessories, the most noteworthy thing is her lack of tact, of nobility, the hardening of her extremities. Beyond that, she transcends the original. She's not a clumsy imitation. In her presence, not even the boys are so monstrous.

Yedra watched her from one side, with her pagan incredulity. She didn't enjoy the show. She doesn't understand its significance. She's been taking the whole thing in silence but is insulted by the swaying of the dirty bag of sawdust, that's what she calls her.

This strange creature can reverse the perversion of the family. Therein lies her value. I'm happy with this new Lana.

I've lost interest in my soulless games. Now I know love. Fate's glorious gift.

Man's (Almost) Personal Diary

Friday 29th

Sexual Encounter, Intensive

11:00

Today Father made us pose with Norma. The machine is dull and doesn't get aroused. It opens its mouth but lacks saliva. Being dry isn't a turn-on, Father said.

He's tired of society photos. In art there's greater license. So he's playing the surrealist. He called Norma and dressed her up identical to the other.

"Natural anatomy is superior."

"But she's got a polio leg?" Fredo knows how to wound.

"It's not contagious. She got the vaccine."

"She repulses me," I point out.

"Take a look at yourself," Fredo fired back.

"Her leg looks like a snake," I said, because she couldn't hear me.

"That's her charm. This girl is an exercise against boredom. With her, tedium is unlikely," Father outdoes himself.

Norma was beautiful. She came in wearing a little nightie,

holding hands with the other. She looked at me and I felt an urge to settle down with her. Stake my claim. But reality produces a kind of metaphysical opposition in me. It sounds difficult, but it's easy to feel.

Then Yedra set the stage. She spread out a dirty flag across the floor and said Ready. For sweat.

"Can you get me the sword?" Father got his old Leica.

"With objects it's a different price," Norma said.

"No problem. You keep track," Fredo touched her and she jumped.

"Your hands are freezing."

"Everyone on the floor," the Colonel can't help himself, it's his military temperament.

Lana and Norma lie back on the flag. They're not wearing underwear. That patriotic double pubis made me feel a longing for revolution. I was instantly erect. Against my will and methodical spirit, I was positioned on all fours.

Geometry is a double-edged sword. There we were, on that white and sky-blue world. A universe of wreckage, a whore from the outskirts and the two of us: the culmination of that entwinement. Our bodies forming protests, demonstrations, strikes. Father's camera like death's eye. Blinking every so often, shuttering and clicking.

Yedra had retired, in case someone came to the house. To play the part of warning bell.

At some point, Norma's little leg appeared on my neck. I thought I'd die in that instant, the artistic sclerosis was asphyxiating me. And yet, I persevered. I told myself to transcend the moment.

The girls kissed me simultaneously. Fredo tensed. He didn't

know how to pace himself and Father's camera demanded it. The light was low.

"There, hold it. A little longer. Don't breathe."

"It's like you're taking an X-ray," Fredo wanted to get on with the groping, I didn't let him.

We shot two terrifying rolls of film. Lana decided to sing a hymn to the fallen flesh with Norma's voice. I fainted before it was over.

When I came to, Fredo was still there. Like that dinosaur.

Against the Object,
Retracted Ballad

Everyone is asleep. I'm in the darkroom. After inspecting the machine, I've concluded that it's too refined. It doesn't look like Domingo's work. Staring at its flat stomach, I feel a shiver. A thread of hatred.

Earlier, Yedra came in wearing a nightgown. I was tempted to hide, not remembering I'm invisible. Yedra walked up to Lana and spat on her. Then a burst of mocking or furious laughter contorted her lips. Lana didn't react. If I'd still had eyes, I would've wept.

I hadn't felt like myself at all in recent days, drifting off to sleep constantly. Now I look for any distraction I can find to keep myself awake. I'm trying to concentrate. I've come up with an interesting exercise. I look at Lana and plant the idea in her that I exist. Once or twice I thought I saw her wink her left eye. She knows I'm watching her.

I smelled her hair today. It's dry, coarse. It appears to be dyed. Sometimes I feel bad for her, but other times I look at her and feel nothing. I can't deny her beauty, how natural she looks. She sleeps on that cold little bed Domingo made for her, like a Soviet princess. But she snores.

In a different context, I would've celebrated the Colonel's genius. He's managed to transcend his own limitations. I thought he would give up when I torched Photovoltaic Lana. And yet, this Lana is superior.

But it's too late now to congratulate him.

I wander lazily through the house and the world, trying to locate the details that will release me. I don't want to wait any longer for my date with the infinite. My earthly self is decomposing.

Sick of all reality, nothing feels right to me. I lack body—or is it a lack of memory? Before, I was a torrid girl. Now, a failed little woman. Halfway dead, neither cooked nor raw.

From the beginning my life looked like it was over. I went around holding death by the hand like a lover. And then, along the way, one man died and another was born of me, with two masters atop his neck. A child of a double consciousness, or should I say a consciousness squared?

What Lana Says

1. Beauty is sinuous. And it gets used up.
2. Sharp, cloying mouth, I feed Domingo. But it's only Monday.
3. Tepid nipple. A finger in my dry vagina. Both exalt me.
4. Am I a cave or a monument? I was something once. I remember the void, the undrawn before.
5. I dress like her and suffer her. Falling from the bitter deathbed.
6. A faint odor of rot perturbs me. A stitch in my neck.
7. I see her die every time I shut my eyes, shut my legs. Her death fucks with me. With all of us.

Tatters of Life, Saeta

I went to visit my grave and discovered the headstone was never finished. They couldn't be bothered. The date of my death was unfinished.

Buda is the only one who loves me. Last Thursday, I watched her flip through the photo album. Staring at what was left of us. Two polariods that never fade. Afterward she wrote in her diary. She addressed me as if I were alive.

Monday 13

It was six months ago today that we took that trip to Carlos Paz. Remember? It was too cold for vacation, but you wanted to get away from the Colonel. I liked it when you didn't pull your hair back and tie it up so tyrannically above your nape. I liked it when you let it down. We went to have tea in a secluded retreat and you started to cry. It was the first time I'd seen you like that, so vulnerable. I didn't know what to say because, honestly, I just thought you needed to lighten up. Your downcast eyes and childish pout made me love you more.

What's become of the things you told me, I don't know. I can't work up the nerve to ask. The Colonel seems sad without you now. But I never really trust him. Maybe it's his nature as military man, I always think he's hiding something. Behind the smile, the saber.

Men are obsessed with things they can touch.

Tuesday 14

•   •   •

Wednesday 15

Pay health insurance.

Lana Untamed

Taking advantage of the absence of the Colonel and the *deformes*, Yedra draws the blinds and lights some candles. She sits in the middle of the dining room and repeats my name maniacally. Calls to me, summons me.

"Come to me, Aurora. I am your servant."

Her naivety makes me smile. Her jowls quiver as she says my name. I blow out the candles like it's my birthday and she tenses up, frightened.

I sit down beside her to think about me. I almost don't remember myself anymore. Sometimes, a nebula settles over my memory. Death eliminates the past first. Consumes what was and to come. Extinction in installments. The present is the last bone to cling to, the most enduring. The soul's power cannot be conjugated. To be is infinitive.

With Yedra, there's no going back. The cheap perfume on her neck keeps me partially there and I am grateful to her for that detail. I can be awed by anything, physical things most of all. The senses take a long time to forget.

She says to me Don't go, takes off running. I follow her to the darkroom. She knows it. We continue our morbid dance. She shakes Lana and I hide at a distance. The shock bowls me over. The truth revealed. She and Lana look at each other. Yedra lifts her chin and tries to find me with crazed eyes.

"Don't be frightened, Aurora. And you: don't move."

"Who're you talking to?" Lana says with an insolent gasp. "Don't you dare touch me."

"This is the cause of your death."

Yedra tries to find me, not knowing where to look. Lana puts a hand over her mouth, grabs her from behind, and shoves her into the closet. Yedra screams. The other is undeterred. She locks the door. I hear her footsteps move off toward the kitchen. Lana opens the blinds and starts to sing.

Yedra speaks as if she can see me. And she tells me the truth.

Making Themselves Heard

I listen to her voice from inside the closet, muffled by the coats. She speaks without stopping to breathe, without thinking, shot through with rage. All the while, Lana's song in the distance. On the far side of the house, she sounds happy.

"The Colonel is a liar," Yedra shouts. "After Photovoltaic Lana, he tested another unsuccessful model. We scrapped it. This Lana is made of flesh."

Yedra pounds furiously against the door and I go dark. Lana sings, her bored little voice drifting down the hallway.

Febo asoma y a su paso. It can't be true. This machine doesn't have a heart. Did I die at the hands of an actual adulterer? Did the interloper and the deadbeat really plot my demise? I approach the android. I didn't pay enough attention to her. I never really liked household appliances.

But one night I was struck by her posture. Lying on the ground beside the Colonel in the courtyard, looking up at the stars. She laughed. He said something frightening: I love you.

Lana is in the bathroom, applying my products. She makes faces in the mirror. Without makeup she doesn't look human. Her skin is gray.

Doubt slithers across my soul like a snake. I want my Hamlet.

Ideas That Keep Me Occupied

Lana in the role of God: a mindless animal.
Now that I'm unmoored, the void submits to me.
Death reflects and life absorbs.
Everything is confused: parody of the stupefied state.
Form and purpose are one and the same.
Without form there is no direction.
Life is victim of its own success, that's why it fails.
Death doesn't end, the hereafter is infinite.
The self, a bucket of warm water.

Fantastic Vision

Using my lipstick, Lana paints herself a tempting and excessive mouth. It looks like a floret of flesh. It's not ugly, but there's something strange about it. The palettes—too starkly contrasting—form a dark tunnel in the middle. That and the bags under her eyes give her a disturbing cannibal air.

She takes out a white wig and puts it on. Her real hair is black and stiff.

I feel her heart beating deep inside, hidden beneath her soft breasts.

Yedra pounds on the closet door and the Colonel comes in from the street and lets her out.

"What're you doing in here?"

"Lana Carne locked me in."

"What'd you do to her?"

"Me? It's either her or me," she wails. "You have to choose."

"Don't endanger yourself," Domingo says with the eyes of a man disgraced.

Yedra walks away without responding, calculating. When she gets to the landing on the stairway, as if she could see me, she says:

"Take care of it yourself. It's your problem. I'm done for the day."

People are cowards. I don't know how to proceed without a body. I need someone to move for me.

Deliriums like Stones

Last night I whispered my displeasure to ManFredo. Fredo's part didn't understand. Man woke up. He looked like a sleepwalker. He put on his robe, walked to the darkroom, and tried to open the door. Locked. He was about to lean an ear against the wood to listen, when he heard the Colonel's slippers. Approaching. Domingo was carrying the breakfast tray in his hands. Two coffees with milk and four pieces of toast with cheese. Man hid, disconcerted. The Colonel turned the key and entered the room with a distracted air. He didn't close the door.

Fredo woke up while Man was spying. Lana and the Colonel ate on the rug. One of her legs on his chin. They talked and laughed, in their improvised picnic.

Fredo smiled, not grasping the scene. That beautiful body toying with Father was too feminine not to be real. Autonomous and corporeal. He kicked the door open with a bang. The Colonel choked. Lana's lips parted; she supressed a hysterical little scream. Man recognized her. She wasn't wearing the wig, but it was still her.

"Norma?" he stammered.

"What?"

"Respect my privacy, dammit!" the Colonel bellowed.

"That's what I say," Fredo answered with excess irony.

"It's one thing to platonically love a tool and something else entirely to cheat on Mother with a person," Man ventured, clutching his hemisphere. It looked like he was about to explode.

"Your mother's dead and I am not a person," she taunted.

"Shut your mouth," Fredo screamed. "Know your place, be silent."

"Don't take that tone with her. We're going to get married," the Colonel announced with aplomb.

"What're you saying, Father? Don't be ridiculous!" Fredo said, stealing a piece of toast.

The Colonel swung at him but lost his balance.

"Don't make me get the gun!"

"If she wants to stay, let her stay. But she has to be for all of us," Fredo said, leaning in to kiss her.

She let him and then bit his lip. ManFredo started bleeding. The Colonel got the gun.

"Nobody move! Are we going to calm down?"

Man got nervous and tried to take over the body and its actions. This resulted in a frenetic dance that frightened the Colonel. Lana screamed stop, stop, stop. That's all she could come up with. Domingo pulled the trigger.

The ManFredos dropped to the floor.

Thirst for Heaven

I get hypnotized watching the bathroom faucet drip. Or the shadows the city casts on the courtyard wall. The moon bursts into my house every night. Reality doesn't interest me, it drags on inexorably, like a movie I've already seen. Always the same actors, and she, dressed up to torture me. I feel alone, horribly alone.

I tell myself it's almost over. Maybe I should leave this house. Family is a kind of hell.

Maybe I should go to the cemetery, but there's nothing there that interests me. Death must be elsewhere, occupied. She forgot to come for me. I'm like a sweet-sixteener stood up by the devil.

The Wing is Cloth

Umpiérrez removed the bullet and then announced to the family:

"One hemisphere is dead. If you like, we can take this opportunity to make aesthetic improvements."

Yedra started to cry. The Colonel and the substitute waited in the other corner. Buda smoked in the doorway.

"When he wakes up, we'll know which one survived. In the meantime, you should all get some rest. You don't need to be here."

The hospital frightens me. Halls full of beings like me. Dead in the waiting room, at the counter, by the coffee maker. I go with Buda to watch the rain falling on the sidewalk. The sky breaks and furrows with a terrible flash of lightning. People run and that's how I can tell the dead apart from the living. They drift along slowly, vaguely disoriented but unbothered under that deluge.

I fear I've caused a misplaced sadness. My sons suffer while Lana consoles the Colonel.

The police are increasingly suspicious of my family. Every so often, an inexplicable accident. First the wife, now the son. Who's next? Everyone had to make a statement, but first they got their story straight. They were cleaning the gun and it went off by accident.

Domingo looks devastated. Wrinkles scrawled across his forehead. Yedra prays maniacally, an unintelligible babble. Buda thinks of Man, hoping he survived. I curl up beside her. She's my last refuge.

All of a sudden, I remember the violent dream that preceded my pregnancy. Me, in the bathroom, watching a proto-being emerge from my vagina. A horrid creature, a plastic-wrapped embryo, floating in the toilet. Suddenly, the plastic turned to glass and the creature mutated into two strange fish. One vivaciously long, the other quick and colorful.

I'm regressing. At times I feel like a little girl. My first days as vivid as my last.

Born of the Sun

While everyone else awaits the outcome, I revisit my life. A corner full of dead images. I see my childhood. The old house that collapsed. Its cracked sheet-metal roof caved in during a hailstorm and the rest of it bulldozed to make a parking lot. The school isn't there anymore either, a tree along the sidewalk is the only thing I recognize.

I move down the hallway toward the bedrooms as if slipping between parked cars. There's nothing personal left in the world. Everything is external. It's like I never existed.

Memories of the dwarf on the stage make me laugh. I was already dead then, so dead and so conscious. Now I'm a tubercle in my own head. I walk, wearing myself like a little hat; instead of a feather, an idea. Glowing, I wave to the audience. Sometimes I lose myself and then reappear, struggling onward like a starving organism.

Grotesque sensation that of being run through. We sit to keep from seeing, but time wins. It applauds you with one hand and erases you with the other.

I no longer am. And so what? I'll anesthetize myself soon.

Recapitulation

"No change: the third hemisphere died. Though he's still divided, he's more democratic now. Each has his own hemisphere. Oh, I removed some bone. And forget the plural. Scientifically, Manfredo is one person."

The group sighs with relief. The words bounce around in my ears as if on a ping-pong table. I don't grasp their meaning. The sea of language mingles with the summer heat.

The floor is damp and I look down at everyone's feet. The Colonel's have worn his shoes out unevenly and throw him off-kilter. Lana is wearing some Bordeaux sandals my sister gave me a long time ago. Yedra, threadbare flats. The old woman has also worn her soles unevenly. She's always listing to the right, as if in a tailspin.

The nurses glide soundlessly forward in white plastic sneakers, they look like figure skaters of misfortune. Full of blood and giggles. Pirouetting on tiptoes, injection at the ready, scanning for a patch of flesh to shoot up with that narcotic liquid.

All of a sudden, a pair of bare feet call to me. Their owner is staring at me. And smiling. I don't recognize his face.

From on High They Will Come

"Aurora?"

"Who's that?"

"It's Horacio. The accountant. Did you already forget me?"

"No. But you were dead."

"For some reason, I'm still here, prisoner of the form."

"You too? Why here?"

"This is the room where I was admitted. Number 257. You never came to visit."

"I thought it was quick. Your death hit me really hard."

"I suffered for months. I was waiting to see you."

"Is that why you jumped off a third-story balcony? Seemed unlikely."

"I always held out a little hope."

"I didn't know you'd survived."

"You've changed. You don't look like yourself."

"It's been years."

"Time is for the living."

"So, were you waiting for me? What about your wife?"

"I'm a magnifying glass. You were the world."

"You're lucky. Mine is empty."

"That diminishes me."

"Will you die now that you've seen me?"

"Probably."

"What can I do?"

"I want to kiss you on the lips."

"I haven't got any."

"I know how. Come here."

I feel a warmth deep inside me, an I-don't-know-what somewhere. Horacio, or the idea of Horacio, overlaps with me, settles inside me. He darkens in my person, in death. I'm a black hole.

"Now I must go," he says more slowly, from somewhere I can't see. "Don't take too long. The world is nothing. The truth is on the other side."

I'm alone. For a moment, I thought I'd die too. Horacio vanished as if he'd never existed.

I miss him. The wreckage of our love won't soon be eclipsed.

A Key

That moment with Horacio left me sad. It'd been so long since anybody had looked at me. Since anybody wanted me, since I'd been good for anybody. To exist for another. What a mystery. I kept Horacio here. But who keeps me? Why do I stay? If nobody mourns me but that man who's now gone. Life is a skein and one of my strands is missing.

It's not the boys. Even though now—beside them as they sleep, with only one head, now that they're beautiful—I remember how I made them suffer and I hate myself.

I asked a thousand times for night to come, so I wouldn't have to see them. I wished they belonged to someone else, so I could laugh at them. I dreamed I ran away and woke up weeping. The Colonel on one side, the two of them on the other. I couldn't count on Yedra either; she didn't accept her role as domestic servant.

The day I left for Europe with the Colonel, Man wept and clung to my dress. He still had a head all his own then. His sad eyes stayed with me the entire trip. But I shook him off. If Fredo hadn't intervened, I would've kicked him.

"Who do you think you are?" he said scornfully.

"Your mother," I said, not thinking.

"You wouldn't know it."

The Colonel's hand went to his holster, a kind of threat.

"Go in peace," Yedra yelled, excited. "In America, *deformes* go unnoticed. Here, it is how it is. Not like in Europe . . . There, with the right ancestry, *deformes* thrive! Viva anarchy!"

"Quiet. People will notice."

I wanted to float away like a helium balloon. That's all I am now, but I cannot.

Committee: Toccata and Fugue

The *hipertensas* smile more than before. My portrait presides over the room, but nobody looks in my direction. The jowls and bags under their eyes look like soap bubbles. The sun comes out, they drink tea and lay out the future across the table. It could be said that the world runs better without me.

"Aurora was a dictator in black panties," says a young woman I don't remember. "I give you Ludmila, her brilliant successor."

Applause, nervous coughs. Clinking teacups.

"I promise to be cordial and accessible. Lead me not into mutation and deliver me from evil, amen."

Applause for the witticism and distribution of prayer cards. The room is hung with streamers. President Ludmila. They bring my face down off the wall and hang hers, smiling with satisfaction. But it's not a good portrait. You might even say that time is running out for that face, that body. It's shaky and its circulation blocked at every turn. It pains me to witness her debacle, but, in effect, she collapses on top of the strudel, while I'm looking at my portrait on the floor. She comes crashing down like a monolith. Forehead into a spoon, breasts smashed against the teapot. Screams, chairs tipping over, whinging.

The *hipertensas* lose it, dramatic spikes in blood pressure. The young woman gets flushed. A nurse lays her down. Luckily, they're in a hospital.

They are unable to move Ludmila. She's gone stiff on the table. Not a breath of life in that hunk of dry flesh. A group tries to move her up to intensive care, but can't get her on the gurney. They decide to transport her on top of the table. Ludmila looks like a Christmas turkey. Glistening and immobile. They carry her out and she expires while they're waiting for the elevator.

I stay to greet her, resigned off to one side. Waiting for her path to intersect mine in this nonplace.

But Ludmila passes by as if I weren't there.

"Welcome," I say. I'm like the doorman to the great beyond.

She doesn't see me. She's nobody now. A soul that vanishes. She moves on to the other world without a layover. One way to nothingness.

I hope they put my portrait back on the wall.

My Dear *Deformes*

When you read this letter, I'll be gone. I've decided to leave. I only stayed out of habit. But since debauchery—the little whore—moved in with us, the world has turned into a cabaret and I'm left out.

Your mother is not at rest. She's still here. Heartbroken. I'm not saying the false android must die, but the great cleanse is coming.

I leave you my gloves.

Fantastic Battue

The sound of desire comes from my bedroom. Lana and the Colonel are taking pleasure in each other's bodies. She smiles as she rides. He lets her trot in silence, eyes blank, empty. I sit or stand off to one side. What I mean is that I settle in to observe this amorous routine as if it were something established. When they bite each other, they do it for me.

This girl's flexibility never ceases to amaze. She looks like an acrobat, or a hoop tamer. Domingo is round like a meatloaf. Pink rolls abound in every direction. That scene reminds me of being alive. Of Horacio. I don't know if I fully appreciated the fact of breathing. I sealed my fate without a thought for what it all meant.

Laughter floods me as I discover the Colonel's limitations. He breathes raggedly, turns yellow, and whispers ay ay ay in the acrobat's ear. I am free. I don't have to deal with a bunch of ridiculous organs.

"Domingo!" Yedra screams from the hallway.

"Can't you tell that I'm busy?" he replies, coming down from desire like an elevator.

"I just want to say goodbye."

The Colonel doesn't answer. Yedra is carrying a suitcase. When he opens the door, the Colonel has on one of my robes, covering his sex.

"Where are you going?"

"I can't take it anymore. The boys will be fine. You seem entertained."

"Do you need money?"

"It's not about that. I'm taking what's mine."

"All right. If you need anything, let me know."

"Is that all?" Yedra fires off, her eyes gleam with rage.

Yedra pushes the door open and falls on Lana like a sharpened pair of scissors. The tamer defends her arena with efficiency. One of her legs is caught. The Colonel tries to separate their limbs, but makes a mistake. Whose hand is this? Yedra's mouth is bleeding, from the hate she feels. Lana bites and rips off her braid. Yedra bolts before the Colonel's stunned eyes. Like a wild horse. Her hair gets caught in the throat of the acrobat. All of a sudden, Yedra's muscles tense up in the area of her chest. After a few seconds, she drops to the floor. A nail file protrudes from her heart.

Yedra sees me. We're motionless, two walls of time.

Domingo removes the nail file and she returns to her body, on the bed. Lana runs to the medicine cabinet. Yedra is lost to me.

Alone again.

Distant Condor

I thought Yedra was coming to join me. But no. She's still breathing. The wound just damaged her left armpit. They lay her down on Manfredo's bed.

I think curiosity is all that keeps me here. My family mixes with other memories, but always stands out in the sum of activity. My whole life is pure past, except for them. Beings full of urgency. They don't let me do the great revision. Hold still!

I open the door to the courtyard with difficulty and I remember the boat that brought us here. A boat is the sound of a spreading fever. I see Father, stare him in the eyes. Aged irises, younger than my death. A man with anguish etched in every wrinkle. A face in a rush to vanish.

I wish I could've followed him through backstreets of the city center, from Retiro to his life without us. That man was not happy. But who is?

My life stretches out in every direction. I can settle in any corner and conjure myself. I occupy this house as if it were a body. I'm the ambient temperature.

The New Boy

The boys came home today. The loss of the third hemisphere isn't even noticeable. But this young man in the bed doesn't resemble any of them. Neither Man nor Fredo nor the synthesis of the two. The result is an amnesiac man of striking beauty. Umpiérrez made a few slight modifications and that face, like a rib, was transformed into an archetype of symmetry and mystery.

They brought him home in an ambulance and the Colonel told them to put him next to Yedra. Lana Carne looks at him with ravenous delight. She can't help but lick her lips.

The young man asks for water and she runs to fetch him a fresh glass. Yedra is in the next bed, in a stupor. She's been administered excessive painkillers for the severity of her injury. Lana is keeping her doped up.

"You, I don't remember you either," my son says.

"I'm Lana."

"Family member?"

"No more talking now, love. The pieces will all fall into place."

"And the woman in the next bed?"

"Nobody. Pay her no mind. She's delusional."

Manfredo recovers in silence. Lana has set up a screen between the patients. But Yedra, condemned to morphine, floods the room with snoring at all hours.

He wonders who he is, where he is, why there aren't any pictures on the bedside table. But it's still hard for him to focus. A tightly wrapped bandage holds in place an implacable headache.

Lana walks around scantily clad, thinking of what to say to him. Of what not to say.

I sit down to take in the scene, intrigued by the phenomenon. Life is made all alone inside this house. The world doesn't enter in. What happens outside these walls matters to no one. History, medicine, family, death, all dwell within. And they generate a metaphysics of their own.

Sometimes I see it all from overhead. The screen like a net, Yedra and Manfredo, the detritus of a sick tennis game. Lana is the ball.

She comes and goes, pale or wrathful, stuffed into my clothes, wearing my old perfume, pretending to be me. Acting out my life while I play dead. She gets a promotion. From object to protagonist. I act as judge, that is, at a remove.

Fixed Direction

The Colonel is disconcerted. He doesn't know how to live with his lover and this new son who regards him suspiciously. So he opts for isolation. The mechanics of his little room. Of creation.

His mind wheels. His old games, the ardor for Lana, start to dwindle. Sometimes, he passes by Yedra's bed to read her a few paragraphs of his notes on basic mechanics. She looks at him entranced, as if listening to a love letter:

"A clock ticks due to a routine of the system. In articulation mechanisms, the operations or phases occur in segments. Not with valves, camshafts, drive-pins, or rocker arms, but with springs and gears, the clock is a system of calculation with a fixed direction. After twelve-fifteen, it'll always be twelve-sixteen."

And so, when Yedra wakes up and tells Manfredo she's the Colonel's wife, he thinks it's the truth.

"And the girl?"

"Your half-sister. Your father's daughter with his first wife, Lana Carne. Watch out for her. She's no good. A false nettle that dishonors the Berro family."

"And Mother?"

A silence fills Yedra's mouth.

"Your mother suffered a terrible accident. The Fatherland slit her throat like a hungry viper. Ripped out her jugular."

"Where is she?"

"Everywhere and nowhere. She watches over us. Like a god with no believers."

They make me want to materialize, to say it's me. Yedra is deranged. As always. The living can make and unmake themselves on a whim. The dead only unmake. Are unmade.

"What is God?" the new boy says with naivety.

"Don't you remember when we went to Mass?"

"No."

"It's like an old and poorly illuminated theater, where the audience participates in the show, singing or finishing a line, because they already know how it ends. A tragedy with the scent of incense, just around the corner."

"And what's the show about?"

"God is the never-present protagonist. An implacable being with immense power and almost no sense of humor. As if he were already dead, a man in a dress recites pronouncements about the world and tells of the adventures of God's son, a sad boy, half naked and profoundly lonely. He tells a different part of the story every time, to keep the people coming back."

"And the boy's mother?"

"They used her up and left her out, but you can light a candle to her. She's well dressed, as if for a party. They knocked her up without touching her, immaculately."

"How'd they do that?"

"That's one of the show's never-revealed mysteries. At the end, the man in the long dress, who cures without remedy, drinks a little wine and everyone lines up to ingest a circle of paper they call the host."

"Weird."

"That's why we stopped going. Besides, everyone gave us bad looks."

"Us?"

"Yes, you were different back then. And people don't like things that are different."

BudaSalute

She's come to visit the *deformes* and finds a stranger in their place. She looks at him with mistrust, as if they'd brought the wrong person home from the hospital.

"What's your name?"

"Manfredo."

"You sure?"

"That's what they tell me."

"What was your mother's name?"

"Aurora."

"And your father?"

"Colonel."

"Who's snoring on the other side of the screen?"

"Yedra."

"Who's the sinuous girl who let me in?"

"The Colonel's daughter."

"No. Can't be. She must be a nurse. Or a whore."

"She's from the Colonel's first marriage."

"Impossible. I'm a member of this family and I've never seen her before."

"That's what Yedra said."

"The horror! So he had a daughter with another woman?"

"Apparently. Who're you?"

"Your aunt Buda."

"Tell me something about Mother."

"She was an intense woman."

"An anecdote."

"Tomorrow I'll bring the photo album. You and I are going to avenge her."

"What for?"

"Pace yourself. Let's take it slow."

"Am I going to die?"

"No. The odd man out here is your father."

"Buda."

"What?"

"I wish I were someone else."

"Happens to the best of us. Rest now."

Vitriolic Secrets

A new development. Yedra has become intermittent again. At times, she's with me. She looks like a Christmas light, flickering on and off. Lana is to blame for her grievous state, she's not giving her the right medication. The wound is already scarring over.

When she appears on this side, she winks at me. I never expected complicity with Yedra and yet here I am at her bedside, awaiting the rendezvous.

Lana is focused on her desire for Manfredo. Last night she slipped into his bed.

"What're you doing?"

"To keep you warm."

"I'm fine, thanks."

"You really don't remember me?"

"You're my sister."

"No. Not your sister. Kiss me."

"I don't like how you smell. It reminds me of something ugly."

"You didn't think so when we were together."

"When was that?"

"That one night. You came to my room. It was raining.

You were soaked. Don't you remember? Your mother was still alive then."

"Impossible."

"You prayed for her to be gone, and the heavens listened."

Just then, the Colonel enters the room and interrupts. Manfredo freezes. The screen keeps the Colonel from seeing Lana in the bed next to him. She clings to him like a tick.

"Yedra, are you sleeping?"

"Yes, what's going on?"

Yedra sees me for an instant. I reach for her, try to touch her. She dissolves between my fingers.

"Be quiet, Domingo. Aurora is listening."

"Don't be ridiculous."

"Colonel."

"What's that, Son?"

"Can you come here?"

"Not just yet. Hang on."

Lana takes advantage of Manfredo's confusion to slip out of the bed, straighten her clothes.

She picks up his empty glass from the bedside table and heads for the other side of the room.

"Ah, there you are," says the Colonel, not looking at her.

"You two talk in peace," she says, and shuts the door gently.

"I'm afraid," the Colonel says when they're alone.

"Of what?" Yedra leans in close to his lips.

"Did we make a mistake?"

"Excuse me," says Manfredo, sitting up in bed, clouded in doubt. "I feel dread and I don't know what it means. I'm filled with an overwhelming sense of monotony."

"Relax, Father will take care of everything."

Doctor Heine

Domingo invites Silvia over to evaluate the new Manfredo. They walk across the bedroom to the far side of the screen. Yedra is in the depths of delirium, trying to talk to me.

"Aurora borealis, heavenly and elusive, forgive our wretchedness!"

"What's wrong with her?" asks the doctor.

"Old age."

"Ah."

"She's not as bad as she seems," Domingo offers.

"Nurse I am not," Silvia lets slip a cold chuckle, "but her state is worrying."

"She's acting."

"She's good."

"Deliver us from evil and show us the terrible path out of the darkness, for in death one is regurgitated."

"Amen."

Domingo brings her over to Manfredo.

"Here's the boy, a little confused. Maybe he'll remember you. Son, this is the doctor," Domingo winks his eye rudely.

"Relax, I'll take care of him. And don't forget the honorarium."

"I'll leave it on the bedside table."

"Please. Save me the hassle."

"Of course."

Domingo walks out without leaving the money. She notices and clicks her tongue in displeasure.

"Good afternoon!" the doctor almost shouts, as if Manfredo were deaf.

He looks at her suspiciously.

"Who are you?"

"Let's start from zero. My name is Silvia, yours?"

"Everyone asks the same thing. Another woman already came. She said she was my aunt. Everyone lies."

"Okay, very good. Let's play a game. I'll say a word and you say the first thing that comes to mind."

"Not interested."

"Father?"

"Pendulum."

"Mother?"

"Ellipsis."

"Yedra?"

"Button."

"Manfredo?"

"No."

"Life?"

"Shit."

"Sex?"

"Death."

"Illusion?"

"God."

"Past?"

"Smell."

"Great! How do you feel?"

"Same as before."

"In other words?"

"Bored."

"And what?" Silvia looks at his shoes.

"What are you looking at?"

"Your shoes."

"They're not mine."

"And what're they doing there?"

Manfredo doesn't answer. He doesn't find the doctor attractive. Plus she smells bad. Too much perfume. She reeks of poorly washed genitalia.

"Let me be clear. Your psychosis is cured. Whatever happened to you has erased all vestige of pathology. Your personality changes and disorganized thoughts have been replaced by a state of apathy and slightly anodyne hyperreality."

"And what does that mean?"

"That now you're dull and predictable, but healthy. Get used to expecting little of your imagination. And use those shoes. You're all better now. Anything you want to say?"

"No."

"That's what I thought. Okay, that's it. Tomorrow they'll remove your bandage. I'm off."

"Wait, I forgot something."

"Tell me."

"You smell worse than roadkill. You're ugly and your nipples are like melted rubber. It's painful to witness your slovenly indifference. Your desperation is ridiculous. Thank you, that'll be all."

Her eyes well with tears; her makeup starts to run. She leaves without a word. But now, I hear her yelling at Domingo. She says she won't be back. I hope it's true.

Night of Ignorance

I make inhuman efforts to retain perception. I arm-wrestle death. She shoots me up with this weariness. Sometimes I'm alone and tell myself that none of it is happening. That I invented the world in order to remain here.

In these last stages, for some time now, I feel less myself and more nothing. What I mean is, nothingness invades me naturally. Detail is removed from the table of the possible. My scent fades like an ink stain under water.

High in the Sky, Karma

I find Yedra reading a letter addressed to me. Who knows how long it's been there, hanging like a clothespin.

Aurora,

You had your chance and blood coursed through your body. Now it's my time. You never understood the Colonel, never gave your son affection. Nagging Yedra is the only one who ever respected you, just to oppose me. Your minuscule world hates you.

> *Get out of my way. We, the new generations, need space. Not even the dead want to go. Stand aside for the glory, where you won't block our sun. Casting horrid shadows across our newborn bodies, like cacti without mystery. Ascend with your restless souls and let the human god you invented take care of everything. You'll move on to another landscape, more in tune with your sad madness. An open plain and the ringing of trumpets, a sky pierced with thorns. The frame you deserve.*

> *Follow your disastrous heroes down the road to oblivion. Reality kisses me on the mouth, and I let it.*

Enough with the dead woman's laments and unwelcome lurking. Know your place. A sweet breeze is blowing here, love granted me presence, and I'm what comes next. What you couldn't have now is mine. Electric yet sensate nymph, joyfully I take your place. Your burden is my pleasure.

Stop spying, my dear. I feel the vacuum of your cavities, skull scrubbed clean like a lackluster parade. The show is over. Time to die.

Yours sincerely, Lana Carne

Yedra has decided to end it all. Lana is contagious. Without her, the world would be innocent again. We spent some time together. Her soul's wakefulness is minimal. Not much to say. Her head blinked into view. You have to know how to make peace. To that end, it makes me happy.

Carrying stones of resentment is the labor of the living. And so alive, so incarnate.

We agree without speaking. We keep each other company, like old deathbed enemies. We intertwine our fingers and make promises. We can't wait any longer for fate to come. The tragedy needs a push.

Yedra commits to action. I wait in the shadows.

Closing Minutes

Buda arrives with the promised photographs and reviews my life with Manfredo. They laugh. For a moment, they look like a family. Domingo comes in with a tea tray. He even changed out of his pajamas. Smells good. They say.

They look at the picture where Buda and I are holding a trophy. I don't even remember what for. Their voices are lost to me. I can't grasp the narrative. Their mouths flap, their monstrous relationship with happiness drives me away.

Then, I distract myself with the thoughts of someone in the house next door. Nothing special, I struggle to focus. I catch random words. Trivial but alluring. Words that draw me in but nevertheless fade away and grow dull. What a bore, the word. To speak is to yawn. A word is a failed objective, dust in the dead mouth. An attempt to counteract the grandeur of the silence. The din of the hereafter subsumes any impassioned prayer, any act of language. Between the parrot and the shroud, the parrot always loses.

That's what I'm thinking about when I feel a strange pain. Something stabbing me. I, who experience ever less, feel run through. I don't understand. I feel something wild in my head, a longing in my throat. I turn back to the room.

A curious commotion has knocked the screen to the floor. The teacups stain the rug. A piercing scream is stifled. I see them all in a state of shock. Then, without warning, a wondrous scene unfolds on that side of things.

Not So Pure

Yedra hid one of the Colonel's swords under the sheets, and when Lana bent down to give her a pill, she showed no mercy. She stabbed gracelessly, with both hands. Lana cut off mid-scream, tongue extruded, and collapsed atop the assassin. Yedra rolled to one side and cleanly removed the sword, surveying her work.

The wound exposed a tuft of cotton and some cables. Her heartbeat was regulated by a digital clock. Lana looked like a torn pillow. Her torso cut open, bloodless. Yedra laughed shrilly, like a lunatic.

Now the Colonel seizes her.

"What have you done?" His eyes harden in their sockets.

"Is there no way to fix her?"

"Yedra, undo it."

"My sister was fake?" Manfredo is shocked.

"She wasn't your sister, she was an artificial devil, a disposable woman," Yedra sets the sword on the nightstand, discreetly. As if she weren't the guilty party. She lifts the screen off the floor.

Domingo contemplates the disaster, eyes aflame. His greatest invention. He tries to say something, but a lump catches in his throat. He swallows it whole and throws himself down beside the severed body. His hands tremble, uncertain where to begin.

"I thought she was real," Yedra brightens.

"She depended on the most complex of motors."

"You can buy another. I'll get it for you."

"The poetics are rare."

"What's that got to do with anything?" she doesn't grasp the answer.

Domingo kneels over Lana:

"Give me the sword."

"What for?"

"Give it to me."

Domingo removes the head with one precise cut. He points at it as if it were a globe.

"Some of Aurora's ideas were carefully stored here. Her will to live, her passion, the heat of her fury. The contents of her dorsal anterior cingulum and frontal operculum were installed in the Lana vessel. Before she died, I inserted them in this empty intelligence."

Nobody speaks. The sight of a headless Lana holds some of the horror it hides at bay. That or the ostentatious explanation. What's an operculum?

I feed on that pain. It seems that my death is bound to the object.

"Lana Carne, as I came to call her, was beautiful but stupid."

"Like all the previous ones."

"Nobody wants a woman without reason. Aurora had plenty." Buda doesn't even blink.

"Building a body is simple and relatively cheap. But

animating it is tricky, we still don't know what the Self is, what imbues it with grace. Without the subjective mediation of the spirit, there's no way."

"She was identical to Norma. The same little whore as always, the one from the disgusting photos."

"Women are all the same. And I've reached the end in my work. I declare myself incompetent. Life has no meaning."

"And what did you do with Norma?" Yedra doesn't relent.

"Sometimes we kiss. But it's not interesting. A copy of the copy of the copy."

"I feel sick," Buda is dizzy.

Domingo picks up the sword and threatens suicide. Confusion is the best defense. Nobody move or I'll kill myself! His voice sounds false. The pose is uncomfortable. It's funny. He has to move his head away from his arm to put the sharp point against his throat.

Then, Manfredo gets up from his bed with determination. Puts on his shoes.

"Don't be ridiculous, Colonel. You've achieved a great deal. The bitch is dead . . ."

But he doesn't finish his idea. The bitch Aurora or the bitch Lana? The Colonel throws down the weapon, sobbing. He looks like a shriveled and lost schoolgirl.

"Is it so bad to try to be happy?"

"Just the dalliances of a retiree. Nothing to see here."

"Murderer," Buda says suddenly.

"Who, me?" Manfredo looks at her sidelong.

"No, your father."

"I merely took advantage of Aurora's death. The idea sparked in my mind in an instant. It pained me to see her operculum go to waste. But by God I didn't kill her. How could you think such a thing?"

"So who was it then?" Buda wants the truth.

Their gazes whip around like a roulette wheel. The blame never settles in any one slot. A convention of silence keeps them impassive, until Domingo changes the subject and continues his battery of excuses.

"I did the same thing your mother did with you, Manfredito. A synthesis. You were split before. You had to be condensed."

"The horror!" Buda can't contain herself. "You're all utterly crazy."

"What do you mean I was split?"

"It doesn't matter. I'll show you the photos," Yedra looks at Lana's head, distracted.

"From two, I made one. Poor thing, but it's unfair to condemn me and forgive her. Lana wanted to exist no matter the cost."

"She turned out wrong. Why didn't you use me as the model?" Yedra is a contradiction machine and her glassy eyes are terrifying.

"Stop talking. Put her back together, Colonel. This time without the poetry. She'll be for me."

"What would you want with this pile of shit? You're beautiful now," Yedra is confused and fights to take hold of Lana's head. "You can have a real woman."

Manfredo grabs Lana's head by the hair, as if it were a shopping bag.

"I prefer a trial version. You people are vicious," he turns her to look at Buda.

"Bastard," Buda is about to lose it.

"I'm going to start from zero. Today is day one."

Domingo looks tenderly at Lana and starts to imagine her return.

"I'll find the photographs to make you anew, Lanita."

"What photographs! Burn them. I want a new woman."

"The photographs are valuable."

"Who would want them?" Buda says with a grimace.

"You haven't seen them. Dark art, soft-core porn," Yedra makes a moneymaking gesture.

"I don't want to brag, but I've been approached by a German collector."

"A Nazi? That's all we need," Buda can't believe it.

"That changes everything. If I am the model, they belong to me. Where are they?" the new Manfredo heads for the door.

They all run to the little room. An exquisite complacency starts to come over me. I don't want to see how it ends. Buda doesn't either.

"Let's be dignified," she says, as if intuiting that we were departing simultaneously.

Nobody cares or asks her about that use of the plural. They're busy with something else. The cries are audible, the excitation of bodies. Buda leaves the door open. She blends in with passersby and is lost. I let her go.

The Metal of a Voice

While Manfredo offers dark explanations for what's happened and what's to come, he enjoys the obscene images. Triangles of bodies of distinct materials compose startling scenes. The little whore with her wooden leg and Nine-Volt Lana with her half-and-half body kiss each other, lying in front of a fake sunrise. Or clinging to the *deformes'* old head, on the prow of a poorly painted boat. His cackling wounds what meager consciousness I have left.

"It's hideous," Manfredo shrieks. "So horrible that it's genius. This is worth a fortune."

The Colonel feels indemnified. Yedra offers everyone hot chocolate. Nobody mourns me. This second stage of my death feels less tragic, more grotesque. Of my sons, not a trace. They're an almond in the mouth of the devil.

A final hallucination grips me. Suddenly, I'm inside a head, in other words, a dark room. My instincts cease to pulsate. There's no point staying. My opercula no longer function. I let it all go. I begin to descend.

I leave my family and their endless tragedies behind. I see them tangled in a garden that looks like a toy that's been thrown in the trash. The words of resentment pile up and sprout seedlings.

There are no hymns, not even a throat. The Fatherland is in decline.

Time Runs in Reverse

I descend happily, parallel to the city. I would almost say I zigzag, like an ant that's found its hill. I avoid the primitive world and I see others like me toss flowers, or images of dense petals. They welcome me indulgently to this viscous, humid cave.

I've arrived at a uterus that resembles my house, but inverted. I visualize a table. And suddenly, something orients me to this new perception. The world is this now and the other one has been left above, on the flipside. The hemisphere of the living will be my north. The rest will bloom underground.

Life stamps about on the subfloor and it no longer matters. It's like a muffled party that swallows the guests on the other side of the door. Death is pure insurrection: Domingo, I am beneath your feet.

Ludmila directs the reception and improvises a few words: *Dear Aurora: Welcome to the laconic world of the universal. Death rewards.*

Horacio applauds the contradiction and raises a glass. I hadn't seen him there. With no jacket and his curls flying free, he looks even more beautiful. In his dead—which is to say free—version, he reminds me of Domingo. He says he's given up writing his little notes due to lack of materials. That makes me laugh. Among the dead, the humor is exquisite.

Poor Domingo, slave to the parabola. While in the world, we're tyrannized by banal scenes. Temptations are not real. They must be elaborated. Lana's body, or mine, appears to function like a prolongation of his lost desire. We were his parasite happiness, born to give pleasure to the indolent landscape of his soul. What a feat of imagination, a soldier scientist. A man in love with doubling. A body extracted from celluloid is absorbed by the air. It scatters. Marriage is the same.

At last, true clarity annihilates the veil of existence. I feel liberated from military rule: I'd been welded to its dogmas like a hog to its hide. Morality gets in the way.

Father sits before me. There's no fear in his face anymore. No moustache either.

"Even here, I'm your father," he says as if he needed to.

"We have time now," I say, and I blush with the idea of no limits.

"Did you visit Mother yet?"

"She's here?"

"Yes, the hall of the skeptics."

"Where's that?"

"Nowhere."

We laugh, reveling in the farce. I'll visit her soon, there's no hurry. Infinity awaits.

I sip a delicious wine that tastes of botanic novelty. Of being born. I say goodbye to Buda, mentally. The rest fades on its own: Domingo, Yedra, and the mad boy. Creatures crystalized. A waste.

Time will run in reverse for us. Death is acceleration. Our paths will never cross again.

There are no words for what comes next. Just to add that the living world occurs underground. If I dug into the earth, I could spy on it. But I'm not interested. What I've seen since my death was revealing.

To excise my past and leave it in the ground, to get past the hill, that's my only goal. To be something new. Death valorizes, it's the art of concealment.

Don't follow me. Don't pray for me. Now Mother is unmade.

Norma

1975

Dear Colonel,

It's been a long time and I don't know if you remember me. I worked in your studio in '56. I never had a steady man and your photoshoots saved me from dating. I think you're a visionary, in your own way. But that freak show should benefit me somehow. Funds are scarce these days.

The copies you gave me don't sell, even in the neighborhood. They're too sophisticated, apparently.

You made me play with your son, remember? The split-head and bareback riding motif—so juicy. And that look on his face, as if each eye were seeing a different world. The left, in particular, was terrifying, don't you think?

The other picture, the one with us lying on a faded flag that functioned as a kind of divan, the doctor wanted that one. He likes nature studies. That's what he said. You have to be cultured. I didn't know Umpiérrez had any interest in art. He paid me next to nothing. He says we could get arrested.

The one with the young officer pretending to run me through with his sword sold poorly from the beginnning. It's not that my provocative pose or his exposed body parts turned people off. It's because the image was sad. My body glowed against that Persian rug, but it wasn't enough. My thighs looked strange. And my stunted little leg was unsettling.

I want to buy a house, even just a small one. I heard things are going quite well for you and it would be great if you didn't forget your model. Since I had the baby, I've been trying to lead a decent life. I don't want him to be ashamed of his mother. I took the advice of a cousin and have been making house calls as a nurse. But I can't charge much, because I don't have a degree. If you have digestive issues, let me know.

It's hard to be happy. I prepare remedies for the neighbors, my mind wrapped in dread. Today, as I was mixing an ointment, I remembered you and your family. The petroleum jelly sparked the image. Smell is a path leading into the past.

Your son's bad half tasted like a sty. You made me mount that creature. Rub my sex against the back of that depraved animal. Touch myself in front of the shutter. But there was something sweet in all of it. Your son, Man, was good. We spoke many times. When the other fell asleep.

One day he asked me to bring him a notebook where he could write down his thoughts. He'd filled the previous one. He spent years living inside that mental space that was like a cage, he would say. The only safe place.

It seems that in writing, you discover yourself, even if what comes out is ugly. The excavation of ideas is hard work.

One day he read me a line: *hate is a snail, the internal slime.* I loved it, but didn't understand what it meant.

Sometimes I think my boy is your son, he gets so distracted. You always had problems concentrating. Then he dreams of going down that stretch of lost highway in reverse. Without brakes. There again, the imbalance. On the pavement, me, cut open by the sword. Incredible. Severino feels the blade. The man in the photo slashes me and a lock of my hair goes flying, falls across my face. The hair chokes him, my child, though it's in my mouth. It sticks in his throat and he wakes with a start, in a puddle of sweat. Our dreams are surprisingly promiscuous. Unbearable at times. But he doesn't cry. The boy has a thick skin.

How I conceived him, I do not know. I was so busy at the time. You have to track orgasms. Name and date. But he's yours or your son's. The two of you had exclusive access to my body.

I'm going to take a quick nap and come back, I attended a wake last night and I'm exhausted.

I dreamed of you, incredible. That I kissed you on the beach even though we were in your house. Sometimes, when I was posing, you hung backdrops in your studio and we pretended we were on vacation, remember? I could imagine the sound of a beach that your wife had stitched onto canvas. I never saw her at your house except in a photograph; she was always elsewhere. But she hung in a frame by the door.

Once I crossed paths with her at the zoo. She was with a wild-eyed man who looked like a lawyer or something worse. He slapped her and she started crying, he offered her a hand-kerchief. She ran away. In front of a bush our shoulders brushed, but she didn't know it was me. I was sad. She died not long after, remember?

Congratulate Manfredo for getting the post at Customs. I saw him in the paper with some famous people. His physiognomy has changed so much. I barely recognized him. He had an operation, right? Looks a lot like you know who. Your little doll. I'm not saying he's a poof, but he's got the look.

That thing, Lana, really vibrated, didn't she? Her kisses

shot me full of electricity and, instead of coming to my aid, you abused my flesh. The three of us, stuck together like a train without conductor. And me in the middle, the diner car, coming together in my body. That old woman put an end to the ménage à trois, cutting the power. You paid me extra that day. But I've had nightmares ever since. The shock of the electricity changed me. I learned that energy is infectious.

For a few years, I didn't understand it, I thought it was my imagination. Deliriums. Now, I close my eyes and see things. My head spills over. Sometimes I control it, other times it gets the best of me.

The thing is, the other day I happened to see the two of you in *Siete Días* and bought a copy of the magazine. I was surprised by Manfredito's house. The bedspread in his room, so charming.

I light a candle for all of you and try to focus on happy things. But I can't. The smell makes me sleepy and I can't achieve anything. My lungs are irritated by the smoke. Life went bad and now there's no going back. I want to drink, to dance. Suddenly, I feel an impulse to celebrate all my failures. I put on a record from the past, to match what is coming. For an instant, I'm hypnotized, evoking that moment.

A dense vomit cuts off all lucidity and leaves me sprawled across the parquet on top of my mangled leg. That's how I pass the night.

At dawn, I decide to torch the past. *Siete Días* will burn in the courtyard, drenched in alcohol, flaming like a dark candle.

The wisp of incense rises, further deforming those twisted bodies. Manfredo's image melts into mine and forms a single charred creature. The images compress and flare.

Then two things dawn on me: the past doesn't belong to me,

it's a simultaneous invention. The shame doesn't either. It's universal. We can't save ourselves on our own, Colonel.

I was watching the fire, entranced, half stunned, when a sudden wind came up off the river and began whipping around the courtyard. The flames contorted in a wild dance, twisting toward the house I rent.

The result was dreadful. The boy and I ended up on the street. Severino is cold, Colonel.

I'm coming by to drop off this envelope and if it's all right with you, I'll wait for you out on the sidewalk, around six. If you need love, count on me. We'll come up with something. I don't want a scandal.

Awaiting your affection,
Normita, the model

Severino

1989

Image 1: Broken Silhouette

The boy is always getting ahead of himself. He lives in the ante-chamber of things. Never coinciding with the world. When one advances, the other retreats.

The woman who hired him is named Louise and she collects a lot of dust, that's what she said. All of it has to be catalogued and wiped clean.

Severino doesn't know much, but he's systematically antiseptic. Even his resume sparkles. Since he never finished high school, his past is pure fabulation. A suicidal invention to salvage the present.

Stepping out of the elevator on the fourteenth floor he feels vaguely aroused. The impeccable state of the facilities has given him a slight erection. On the horizon the river looks like a fake skating rink, he told me. He's almost a poet.

Lucrecia leaves him alone. The minutes pass like electric automata. They make him pay for the time. Then, the psychological tests. And he lies. He already knows what they want to hear. If they show him a monster chewing on a leg, it's best to say *Boy with drool on his face.* The heads of black birds fighting over the flesh of their prey become *Kittens chasing a big ball of yarn.*

The intelligence test is the same one we practiced at home. He answers well. *Señora* Louise stops the interview, enters the dining room.

"Good enough for me. Have him come on Monday."

"But he doesn't have good enough penmanship," Lucrecia is indignant.

"The last one had good handwriting, and yet . . ."

Severino is stronger when he gets home. He doesn't feel so worthless anymore, it seems. He'll leave behind the days of misery, the remedies.

I go to bed early. The boy frightens me.

Image 2: Vibration

I arrived with my suitcase and they gave me a room on the top floor. I share that piece of cloudy sky with a nest of blind doves. The first night I barely slept. The constant flapping of their wings frightens me. Birds coming and going in the dark until sunrise.

The bed is too hard and the pillow too soft. I can't help but feel my neck as a strange and inflexible substance. I'm used to the ground level, a low-flying creature, that's me.

I sigh. I want to go down. But I know it's inappropriate. It's not the time for capricious wanderings. Yet. But I imagine going down, master of the luxury penthouse that should be mine. I never had a satin robe or a room of my own.

Life so far has been a futile struggle for something better. Tonight I am closer than ever to becoming someone else. Someone sophisticated.

In the final hour, I dream of a rising river, black saliva like an immense tongue licking the glass of the fourteenth floor.

An erotic rush of rutting birds wakes me. I haven't been taking my drops.

Bitter Perspective

Señorita Lucrecia walks two steps behind Louise, like her other possible self. A slightly shorter shadow, piped into an ochre dress, imitating, without the schizoid grace, the meanness of her mistress. When the *señora* is absent, she grows a couple centimeters taller.

She explains my responsibilities, without making eye contact.

"You must be here without being seen, except when necessary."

I promise to be invisible, to become transparent in order to watch the others—the real people. People with money is more like it.

Lucrecia, the household pet, explains the order I should follow with the artwork. She gives me a notepad with instructions. And takes my document. They have everything, even more than one of some things.

It was either this or growing old in Victoria, with Mother. Despite the frustrations, I hold out hope. I'm of an immaculate pessimism.

Santa Nada, Detail

I'm alone from Monday to Friday. The isolation bores into my scalp and leaves me empty. My washed-out hair frames a sad portrait. I've developed a great facility with nonsense and I spend the days talking to myself, amid the chemical compounds and dead flowers.

If I speak, I don't see. Seeing is exhausting. Staying still, the world ensnares me. It's enough to concentrate for my eyes to be taken. But I'm a homebody. Of limited radius. I've never been out of the great Buenos Aires.

I'm the distillation of what I was. A woman of full legs, bah, one full leg and one half leg. Of generous cleavage and a gift for loss. Now I'm squat and gray, even clumsy. As I girl, I offered up my body until I was able to relocate. I never had a steady man, but the appearance of the Colonel saved me from dating.

Now that I hide the object of desire between legs, love is suspect. I keep a head hidden in the floor, and that's how I touch myself now, sometimes. I run my hand across that broken object to fortify my sadness. But it doesn't turn me on. The arousal is metaphysical, nothing more.

Image 3: Entanglement

I see the stacks of art on the floor and want to break it. It's a provocative collection. Setting off a shrieking whistle in my chest, an alarm. I want to be decent, but a thread of resentment clogs my bronchioles. The frustration is like a tapeworm of air that chokes me and makes me bloom in sweat. Calm down, Severino.

Lucrecia leaves me alone. Then I put on thin gloves. The old smell of the ink and my own malaise cling to my spine. They tickle.

In the end, I sit down and select a series that's seen better days, stitched biomorphic silk: ferns and snakes copulating in a hot entanglement. As I pass a cotton cloth across it, I remember something *Señora* Louise said as if in passing: *I love seriality.* And she wasn't referring to cereal. I pretended to get it. I acted like I understood and then went to the library. I didn't find it.

Ignorance is a garment you never take off.

Object 1: Tasks

When I get up, there's nobody here. I shower and take my time. I have to carefully position the hairpiece. A kind of nest that Mother crafted to hide my bald spots. I fix it in place with pins that blend in with my real hair, and it takes almost fifteen minutes to find the right alignment, the most natural way to situate that lie.

A surprising detail that gives my face a kind of intrigue it otherwise lacks. That and my nasal cavities, visibly larger than normal for a facial structure like mine, which in Mother's opinion—cosmetologist and clairvoyant that she is—make me look like a freak.

I put on the apron with someone else's name stitched on the pocket and go to the kitchen. There's fruit in a glass bowl. Black bread. Loose-leaf tea. I find the coffee and prepare two cups. One to drink with my toast, the other to take with me. I'm always lurking. On the prowl. I shut myself in the archives with Lucrecia's instructions. But I prefer to take inventory.

Revulsion

To the right, in Sector 2, there's a cabinet with many drawers.
Long and narrow like curiosity. Original photographs organized
alphabetically by author, covered with a laminate that time has
turned dry and yellow.

In the drawer marked with the letter H, an erotic magazine catches my eye. *Arte al rojo.* There I see three photographs
by Hans Obren. In one, a young woman toys with a strange man.
A man with a split head posing in a mask. In another, they're
stretched out on a faded flag, like a divan. The young officer pre-
tends to stab her with his sword. It's not her provocative pose or
his exposed body parts that turn me off. It's that I recognize the
woman. Though it seems all wrong, she looks a lot like Mother.
A young version, strikingly similar.

How did she end up there? Those are her thick thighs, but
smoother. The skinny little leg too. Or is it just the distance? I
could be wrong. But I swear the woman in the photograph is
Mother. The man's gaze is split, as if each eye were seeing a different world. The right, in particular, protrudes. Almost edible. An
eye that pops out and wants to be inside the beholder. I cover it
with a finger not to see. Yet I'm captivated. The photographs set

my heart racing. But I proceed to inventory the drawers all the way to Z, as if the photographs didn't exist. My blood pressure spikes. I lie down to catch my breath.

At one in the afternoon, I see myself leaving the archive as if I were someone else. In the kitchen, I find a lunchbox with my name on it. I eat the piece of pumpkin pie thinking about the photographs. Mother is vile. Her past, wild. I imagine her as a kind of wet wriggling eel. I shut myself in the bathroom to vomit. So much shame.

Sensation 2: Poetic Capture

I can't wait. I concoct remedies for the neighbor ladies, my mind cornered. Today, as I was preparing a salve, I remembered the *deformes*. The petroleum jelly triggered the image. That smell always takes me back. If I close my eyes, I see them. My head capsizes with images. Some I control, others no. When this happens, all I can do is pray. Or think about this house, about erotic immolation. The future saves me too. I see it beautiful, drenched in prosperity. Domingo, give me light. A broad view.

I stroke the false head and close my eyes. As if it were mine. I distance myself with her, surrendering to the past. There was so much body in my life, and yet, so little love.

The Colonel only spent the night once. He always left before sunrise. He liked to take me from behind, so I wouldn't see his face. But I hung a little mirror on the wall. Openmouthed he cried. Lana, Lana, Lana.

I remember his fluids running down my spine. Norma, I said. And he kept right on saying Lana.

Image 4: Simultaneous Contrasts

The main hall is full of shiny objects, bottomless boxes, texts without language, and things of dubious logic. The ceiling isn't empty either, things hang down. The most valuable pieces are two steel orbs, two meters each, meticulously polished. If you were to peer up at the surface, you'd see yourself tripled and facedown.

There's a mirrored door, hidden along the back wall. There, the mistress hides her past. *To be avant-garde first we were symmetrical.* She speaks in the plural because she thinks she's important.

She's aesthetically opposed to comfort. Or so she says. Yet she sleeps on goose down. She's got money, yet darns her own socks. Utility bores her. *I only pay for art.* So at night, while she sleeps, Lucrecia takes care of everything.

Louise has a hard time falling asleep. She needs somebody beside her. She's afraid of being alone. Knowing there's someone breathing nearby lets her fall asleep. The other is her antidote.

Coleopterans in the Net

On the first Saturday there's a cocktail party. Drinks all around. Even among the collections. I start setting up for the event early, happy because I only have a half day. When I'm about to go, Lucrecia tells me that I have to stay. That I'm not to eat, just keep an eye on how things progress.

I phone Mother and cancel. There's overtime.

"Put on something elegant," Lucrecia says with a mean smile.

"Elegant?"

"If you don't have anything, we'll go to the *señor's* closet."

The dead man's bedroom is at the end of a carpeted hallway. His shirts are too small, they don't button, but Lucrecia solves that with a plush jacket.

"The *señor* was shrinking. He went down three sizes in a month. Don't laugh."

"No, I was thinking of something else."

"What size are your feet? We'll try these loafers."

The shoes fit just right but make a noise against the floor. I move among the guests like a strand of seaweed, uncomfortable and too visible. Every so often, I take refuge in the kitchen, but there are people everywhere. The waiters laugh at the squelching of my borrowed shoes.

When I go back into the living room, I lose it: my maniacal side emerges. I grab a guest by the wrist to stop him from setting his drink down on a signed original. The man shrieks, making a fuss. He dribbles on his scarf, which, moreover, doesn't match his suit. He fires off a slew of admonishments until *Señora* Louise arrives.

She whispers her rage in my ear: Apologize, idiot. And she pinches my arm. I'm paralyzed. The guy says No big deal, the help doesn't understand. Everyone laughs to smooth things over and Louise smiles like an ailing woman, gaunt and alone. She enjoys the suffering of others. She feeds off these things.

Waiters dressed in pig masks make their entrance, distributing aperitifs. Others file in like lobsters, stuffed in hard plastic costumes. The guests applaud and chew. The masks become indistinguishable. The penthouse fills with pigs and crustaceans, their hides glisten, giving off infectious aromas.

Señora Louise's accountant picks up a little skewer and opens his huge mouth, inserting the entire decapod into his oral cavity, as if his life depended on it; then he sucks the little skewer, his eyes clouding over. Sauce runs down his black teeth.

I shut myself away in the dark sky. There was offense in that *idiot*: Louise knows I'm over thirty. Calling me idiot is doubly violent. She's also calling me a nobody.

I phone Mother. They'll fire me for sure: she tells me to breathe.

When the guests leave, the *señora* knocks on my door and leaves me a tray of canapés in the hallway.

But I'm resentful. When I can't hear even the echo of

laughter, I go out into the living room and pick up a book off the turquoise sofa. Pictures of amputated statues. Colorful phalluses, shapeless nausea.

I throw it in the trash, with the food scraps. Nobody will know. That's how art is—disposable. An instrument of desire, brief and deceptive. A mollusk-like creation in the same category as excrement.

I tremble.

Antennae Pinned Back

Apparently *Señora* Louise goes around always surrounded by a choir of sycophantic fairies. If she yawns, they pretend to be sleepy. If she turns, they turn too.

"She's queen of her clinging hive," Severino tells me over the phone.

I listen with disinterest. One leg aches, or both. Nothing escapes me. I detect particles and signals that move forward or backward. Mine is a spatial thing. A gift for parallelism.

I like it that Severino visits. But he has to take the train all the way to Victoria. Walk to my house. Exchange pill bottles and witticisms with the pharmacist on the corner. Help me with the concoctions for the neighbors.

When he comes, I put the head away. I don't want him to think badly of me. Or to get upset. The boy has a short fuse.

"They shut the double door, but I can hear them snoring," he says.

"Attend to your work, darling," I tell him. "Don't consider their bodies. You can't reveal your true colors yet. Have you found anything of value?"

"I want to earn my place and their trust."

"But keep your eyes open. What's hidden isn't seen. My thing is surfaces."

"I do. I'm the intruder, the spectator of external idiocy."

"Don't say things like that. It'll make you nervous. Are you taking your drops?"

"Yes."

"I don't believe you."

"Then why do you ask?"

"I'm your mother."

"I found a magazine."

"Oh, and?"

"With photographs of a nasty model from the fifties. She looks like you."

"Watch yourself, Severino."

"I know it's not you, because your life was a failure."

"What do you know. I had my moments."

"I'll show them to you. The photographer was Hans something-or-other."

"Please, focus on what matters. Ignore what doesn't. Don't bring me this nonsense. Forget the sideshows."

I hope it's not me. It can't be. The Colonel's name is Domingo, not Hans.

Object 2: Darkness

Night is a cavern that leads to the great deception. I stumble at
the threshold. I read until the sun sinks into the building across
the street. There are books everywhere. Mother donated mine
when I was committed. Now they've come back to me. I learn
art as a noun. The object in space. I sink into an abyss of conceiv-
ing the world as an askew and infinite cube. I study theories of
art and, in the silence of my head, I repeat: *They see the carapace,
not the heart. Objects possess mystery. I have the ability not to know and
to grovel alone in the beauty of the form.*

I see myself as a crack in the mirror. The door through
which things disappear. I think of freeing them from their miser-
able, commercial destiny. I want to be their Ali Baba.

Reflected in the orbs in the dining room, I have powerful orgasms. If I position myself at that precise point in space, my
multiplied reflection excites my consciousness. I have perverse,
simultaneous thoughts. I rub the cloth a thousand times across
each hemisphere, as if in a trance.

I believe I've seen the future. A deformed sword: my sex
extends in opposite directions, like an ellipsis of fury.

Superposition 1

This morning we had a visit from Louise's best friend, Vilma Cohen. A scrawny old lady with a narrow-brimmed hat fixed to her skull. Huge sunglasses that swallow up her nose. She looks ugly behind her glasses, from the side, her eye sockets like dry wells. Neither blinking nor producing liquid. She reminds me of the poorly preserved mantis in the museum of natural history. Her skin finer than carbon paper.

As I walked to the archive, I saw Lucrecia spying on Vilma. She can't concentrate when there are other people in the vicinity. She wants to be now what she imagines she'll become in a few years. Taking Louise's place. Being mistress of that kind of life, sans crow's feet. Lucrecia's not snooping—she's learning.

"You're less substantive . . ." Vilma's hollow voice reverberates off the floor.

"Not at all. Why do you say that?"

"I don't know, because of your recent acquisitions."

"Oh, I thought you were saying I looked thinner."

"No, Louise. I'm referring to your *Mobile View of Hell*. That insipid mobile you brought back from Switzerland."

"The truth is, I don't like it. But Berro got a ridiculous price. And I'll write it off on my taxes."

"What taxes?"

They laugh like sad clowns and Lucrecia thinks they're laughing at her. *They know I'm listening. That's why they talk like that. They're referring to my tits.*

I watch her, hidden behind a pile of plastic tubing, while she observes the other two. The image resembles a Velázquez painting that I can't remember the name of.

Lucrecia withdraws, but lifts the phone off the hook first, so she can listen more comfortably in the studio.

I go to the refrigerator with a dark heart. I'm beginning to feel both pleasure and pain in the same side of my body. I chug water.

I see differently. With perspective. Sometimes my eyes are separate from me.

Lucrecia

When the *señora* leaves, Lucrecia takes the opportunity to dye her hair. She doesn't like to be exposed. Gray hairs frighten her. Like a preview of death. The clock ticktocks in her head and she imagines the minutes pass more slowly under the dye.

Up with the doves, I disentangle the nest and put it on a Styrofoam head.

At a distance, all drama resembles capillary phenomena. Sometimes, people can be reduced to this: something trivial being mistaken for its opposite.

With the right kind of light and perspective, any mosquito can become a vampire.

Sensation 1: Cynicism

I've been walking around with those erotic photographs in my head for a while now. I can't rid myself of them. I took this job for one thing, yet fate wants another. You design your life and death bends it in different directions. Those twists and turns end up yielding distinct vistas, whether you want them or not.

I already witnessed several of the *señora*'s breakdowns. The archive was the latest. But Louise's complaints don't affect me. At first I took them seriously, then I realized they were a performance.

I decide to throw a kind of bottomless, coffee-colored ashtray out the window. Just because. I watch it fly over people's heads and shatter beside a startled little dog. It doesn't hurt anybody, but the action lifts my spirits. I'm a coward. Playing the submissive puppy with Louise increases my avarice for evil.

Something has gone wrong deep in my soul. And there's nothing I can do. I'm not allowed in.

Out of the Cage

On my day off, I take the train. I cross the plaza on a diagonal to avoid the centenary remains of a dead tree. I buy a little bag of peanuts and take out my ticket. I like to move with a distracted air, to make as if I were just one among the many. I hate train cars, the stench, the faces.

I am one, they the many. I don't perceive myself. Everyone smells bad.

I put the peanut shells in my pocket and look out the window. The city disappears behind us, blurred by the wind. First the buildings, then the mansions. The architecture swallows itself until it is reduced to a few squat and dirty houses on both sides of the track. To advance is to fade away. Movement erodes.

I imitate Lucrecia. I bought myself a faux-leather journal to write down my thoughts. I've spent years in the cage of this mental space. The only safe place. Now I've decided to be free, to open myself and decipher the theme. When you write you discover yourself, though what appears may be ugly. The excavation of ideas is a difficult but brief task. Just one or two phrases.

Hate resembles a snail, the internal slime.

Mother waits on the sidewalk, in front of the desiccated loquat.

"What've you got for me?" she asks, giving me a quick kiss.

"Something trivial."

"And the pictures?"

I don't answer. We quickly go inside; she closes the door and looks back outside to make sure nobody saw me come in. People from the hospital stop by on occasion.

She looks at an expensive little book I brought her, while I adjust her peg leg. The wooden one. She stores pieces of old legs under the pine boards of the dining-room floor. If a screw wears out, I lift the hatch and rummage through them. There are several unused left legs. And a false head. The sacred memory. When I'm gone, it keeps her company. Sometimes she forgets and leaves it sitting out on the armchair and I have to cover it up so she won't be exposed.

"Keep an eye on Lucrecia," she says. "She's more treacherous than she seems. Next time, bring me something that belongs to Louise."

"I said no. Her clothes disgust me."

"Listen. I'm the brains here. Loosen the screw a little."

"Don't say that. We're a team. Is that okay, or does it wobble?"

"Let's check, wait to see if it holds. Yes. That's it. Each of us plays our part. Did you find anything?"

"Not yet."

"It can't be that hard. They have everything."

"It seems unwise to hurry."

Sleeping in Victoria is hard. The train passes. And when

it stops passing, we reconstruct it. All night long, steel on steel. Piercing the wakeful mind and obliterating any hope of rest.

When it stops, she snores. She even takes control of the sleep that I don't get, or she navigates nightmares plagued by penises she attempts to exterminate in a kind of macabre tap dance. She wakes as if in a trance. With an ache in one leg. Or the other.

The beds are only a few centimeters apart, a chamber pot beneath. The stink of piss and the incessant trains seem unreal, but we both know that reality is like that—domestic. *A hell for idiots*. Not like it is for Louise or Lucrecia. They occur in the best part of the world. For now.

Little Photocomposition à la Goya

Severino has been in the house over a month and he only just discovered the cameras. His circular pleasures must have been captured. In the middle of a silent orgasm he glimpsed the lens. It caught the light and he tracked the cable to the studio, turned off the VCR, ripped out the tape, and cut it to pieces with some small steel scissors.

Technology escapes me. I can't see it.

The sound of the doorbell brought him back to reality. When he opened the door there was Lucrecia, all aflutter in the company of a man. A phallic. That's how she referred to him. A man generous in intrigue and hair—perfect and straight. That excess was too much for him. Too distinguished.

The scraps of tape in Severino's pocket and Lucrecia, making the familiar gesture for him to remain invisible, kept him from speaking.

It's the first time another man has been in the house. The man's eyes paused on Severino's hairpiece. He knew. Smelled the fake hair. And everything beneath it. Could he have sensed the tape?

Lucrecia and the stranger disappeared behind the mirror.

"There's a man in the house."

"And why do you care?"

"It upsets me."

"Record them," I brighten suddenly.

"You think?"

Severino runs to the studio. Camera four is recording. The bitch Lucrecia scratches herself. She's naked in the dead man's room. Soon, the man appears in the hallway, heading for the kitchen. His legs look like a gallery seat. Did Lucrecia venture out onto that pale balcony?

Severino doesn't know what to do and decides to approach the stranger. To make him uncomfortable. In the kitchen, the man asks his name. The boy says nothing.

"How old are you?" his voice is dry.

"Younger than you, that's for sure . . ." Severino answers.

"And what happened to your head?"

"What's it to you? It's to give me some shade," he mutters, furious.

Why should I explain anything to him, Mother? Irritated, I go to my room and sit in a semiconscious state. My black throat is parched after seeing the balcony man's snake. Terror is always sparked by an image. I imagine everything his underwear conceals, bottled up, liters of thick milk in the shape of a monster. Lucrecia sucks, he lies back. The bed spits them out like a painting that climbs out of the frame and abandons the wall. A suctioning sensation fills the whole space. They look like ghostly medusas floating across the ocean.

I returned to the studio, the tape ended up in my bag. Lucrecia is ours.

Still Life

Coming and going. Returning every Sunday on the train. The inverse direction. When I go to Victoria, Mother is insufferable. I don't stay long. In Retiro, I recover certain composure. Louise's gleaming building, the security guard, and the five elevators eclipse the day's ominous genesis, drinking a maté with Mother and talking about everything we lack.

We happened across the ad by chance, in someone else's paper. And now that I'm actually there—though the job's not done—I want to move on.

I get in the elevator and go deaf for a moment. I arrive on the fourteenth floor, dizzy, but quickly adjust to that happy lethargy. *Living in a skyscraper affords great comfort.* I like to think of myself as an eagle in the offing. Not a sparrow.

I open the door with my own key, enter the code they gave me, and find mail on the table.

A masculine voice stands my hair on end. I walk silently to the studio and look one by one at the images on the monitor: Lucrecia and that repulsive man are lying on the living room floor, next to a revolving sculpture. Totally naked.

I zoom in on their bodies. The man penetrates Lucrecia,

mounts her in a sort of ridiculous scene. He's got his socks on. Lucrecia laughs like an artist while he shimmies his pale, plummeting buttocks. The scene has no dialogue; I watch it as if it were a mediocre movie. But it reminds me of the salacious photos of Mother, or her double. Now they bite at each other like rabid dogs. Things start getting rough.

I wait until the end—the couple's orgasmic cries—to remove the tape. I put it in my jacket pocket. Then, stealthily, I open the front door and make as if I were just coming in from the street, slamming it behind me. I approach the lovers and find them straightening the teacups. I don't get upset like before. I've always been half insect.

I turn my back on them to arrange some catalogues. Then I go up to my room, my heart on fire. The suitcase is filling up.

But that man makes me nervous, even when he's not there.

Sensation 3: At War

On the weekend, Severino brings me the tape of the lovers and I ask the pharmacist's son to make me a copy. I don't want to watch it with the boy. Around him, desire embarrasses me. When he goes back on Sunday with the copy for Louise, I'll watch the copulations in peace.

Along with Lucrecia in bed with that man, the mistress will find a little note.

Get rid of the slut. She's bad luck.
One who knows her well

I'm going to have a drink. I deserve it. Severino is bathing and I can't help myself. I put on the tape. The image is poor. Lucrecia partially blocks the man. Then I see his face.

I release an internal scream, each breath filling me with rage. Is that Manfredo? I rewind and rewatch it multiple times. My heart races with the shock. I'm deranged, I stare at his genitals. It's him. His member is unmistakable. Like his life. Double. Double the normal.

Orgasmic Reiteration, Sketch

The conversation with Mother left me exhausted. I don't know what's going on with her, but from now on, I'm not coming to see her unless I've got something big. Something that might actually save us.

I arrived early and put the copy under Louise's pillow. Then, I went down to buy the newspaper. Lucrecia must have come up in a different elevator, because when I got back, she was already there. I found her with the camera, looking at herself in the oval mirror. On camera like that, she looks like an old actress on the brink of suicide. A turn toward the celestial. She looks at herself and strips off her clothes as if they were a memory. Her body has lost its original form. Lucrecia weeps, staring at her image, motionless, like a marble statue. I zoom in on the mirror. Her eyes are cold. I get turned on. Her sadness gives me a jolt of pleasure. Then my eyes cloud over and, when I look again, she's not in front of the mirror.

A bronze breast strikes me from behind. An original piece Louise bought at auction, perfect for knocking someone out, leaves me unconscious.

When I come to, Lucrecia is wrapped in a satin robe.

"I don't like perverts. Does it hurt?"

I touch the protuberance on the left side of my head. Luckily, my nest of hair absorbed some of the blow. But it's come off and there's blood. Lucrecia looks at me with a triumphant expression as I remove the pins.

"You're almost bald," she says very seriously.

"You're old," I reply.

"Not a word to Louise."

"Not one."

"One tape is missing. Tuesday's. *Give it to me.*"

"I don't have it."

"You have one hour."

"I don't have it."

"No? Well I've recorded everything you've stolen."

"Let's trade."

"You sicken me."

"Half hour, on the staircase."

Lucrecia exits the studio and I follow. Out in the hallway, she turns the corner and I run to Louise's room to retrieve the packet. My temples throb. The explicit scenes will be returned to their owners. The note will never reach its destination.

At the top of the staircase, we exchange a competitive stare, the pleasure withered by the betrayal. We'll both destroy the evidence of our erotic transgressions. But I have a copy.

Harsh is the gaze that falls on the intimacy of others. Pleasure, viewed with tranquility, resembles death. A ruptured blood clot.

When she goes to bed, I take the opportunity to rearrange the inventory. In the laundry room, I check out some garments.

Then, I catch the last train to Victoria.

Mobile Visions

"All crows are black," I repeat, lighting a candle. "What happened to that man from the video?"

"Nothing. He never came back."

"Keep me apprised. He's dangerous. Death stalks his shadow. I see it."

"I'm reading a lot. The meaning of the world ends in me."

"What're you talking about? Stop reading that garbage."

"It alters the art, turns it into something poetic: the uselessness of the void. That's how I am. I rescue them from the claws of materialism."

"Quiet, Severino. Listen to me. Think of things that aren't so morbid."

"Lucrecia's blood."

"Get something big and we'll be done. Forget all of it."

Severino sets a European magazine on the sideboard. He says nothing, but there I am. The boy marked the shameful page. That version of me seems less lascivious beside the plastic flowers. I look at the photographs, not recognizing the poses. The Nazi mustache between my legs is familiar. And it offends me. I put the picture facedown and focus on Manfredo. Try to see. But the candles make me sleepy and I can't. The smoke irritates my lungs. The figures of divination are contaminated. What I did that day, the video of Lucrecia. Sex. Manfredo and the Colonel are a semen stain that never fades. The smell lingers.

I get entangled in the excess of forms; I can't penetrate the city and achieve my aim. I fall asleep without seeing.

Collage

Another nightmare. Cardboard people. Flat cutouts, all stacked up. Corrugated, failed bodies still aspiring to freedom. One tries to escape under the door and I'm forced to use the scissors. The cardboard bleeds a sticky resin. A cutout couple takes me down. I fall across her buttocks, they pin me down and push themselves into my mouth. The taste is awful, makes me want to vomit.

I wake up thirsty. My head hot as the side patio in the sun. Mother was out on her rounds. The house is pungent and I get the spins.

Victoria sticks in my throat, asphyxiates me. Now more than ever.

Image 5: Deterioration

Mother prepares an insipid breakfast that I don't eat, then she shuts the door behind me and I get on the train. I read a newspaper left in the next seat. There it is again: Severino Centeno, wanted. I rip out the page and put it in my pocket. I walk expressionless, my heart shriveled. Reality clings to facts, I try to forget, but it won't leave me be. I shove my last name into my mouth, chew the paper. It lodges in my throat, almost chokes me. But I manage to rise above it, become just plain Severino again. Centeno will be a supressed belch, a kink in my digestive tract.

I caught Mother looking at herself. Her young back in the magazine. Like a taut tongue. Her rosy buttocks and hard nipples enhance the image of vivacious female. Mother was that. After, she looked at herself in the little bathroom mirror. She climbed up on a chair. The loose skin casts shadows. The fabric has stretched with life. You can't feel the animality of her body anymore. Time is bleach. Nothing survives it.

Lucrecia's cries pull me out of myself. They form a line that slashes across the wall. They leave a perfect streak in the wood. Then, gone. The minutes pass like that, like a river breaching its banks.

She's shut in the archive. The repulsive man has her tied

to the table and penetrates her with a hateful look. Lucrecia's demands start to fade. Now she writhes, an expression of disgust painted across her face, turning away from the camera.

I see them clearly, as insignificant as that bumblebee I caught as a kid: I couldn't look away until the end. The sound of its fat little wings fading and its body slamming against the box. Before it died, I moved it. Put it in a jar. I wanted to watch the fall in detail. Seeing someone else suffer is a lesson in pain. Art seems to say something about life, to animate cruelty. Action and reaction. Image is a toy. The LUCRECIA plane vibrates. The man pulls up his pants. He leaves without untying her. He shuts the door.

Suddenly, I panic. He might be coming in here. His footsteps are muffled by the rug. But he coughs and I take cover under the table.

He comes in and goes right to the VCR. He takes out the tape, whistling.

Lucrecia writes on a piece of paper OPEN ME and sticks it over the lens of the camera so he sees. The man's eyes stare at those words for a while, unmoving. Behind the paper he glimpses her glowing silhouette. The suggestion arouses him. The originality makes him smile. He's about to start touching himself when the doorbell brings him back to reality. But then an ant appears on the white wall, walking downward. The appearance of that unexpected body entrances him. He's rapt, nocturnal. The sound of the doorbell is diminished by the sight of the ant, which now, on the floor, climbs up onto the man's shoe. He bends down to follow the insect's trajectory. When it reaches his heel, the ant disappears. Black on black. The insect's intrusive body has led the man to me.

"What're you doing here?"

"Nothing."

The man captures the insect without hurting it. His fingers are delicate pincers. It ends up prisoner in the tube of a transparent pen. Lucrecia and the insect are the same.

"Lepidopterists kill them by pinching the thorax between thumb and index finger."

I say nothing. Louise's voice calling from the door saves me.

"Go deal with her while I clean up."

I sneak out without a word and distract Louise as best I can. Lucrecia strolls in as if nothing happened. I don't see the man again all afternoon.

Silent Film

"The guests will be arriving soon. Only enter the living room to serve the drinks and canapés. Then, disappear. I'll call if I need anything."

"Can I go to bed?"

"Don't even think about it. Wait in the kitchen. We've got a long night ahead of us."

"I'll be watching."

"You don't see anything."

Night stretches out, wraps around them. The man, Vilma, and Louise smoke grass on the rug with a youthful attitude. Despite the persistent pain in her hip, Vilma is sitting full lotus. She takes little puffs, blinded by time and the position of her body.

The repulsive man drinks nearly transparent whisky, diluted with ice cubes. He likes to moisten his mustache on the rim of the glass, to feel that slight dampness. Louise, barefoot, has on a black leotard with irregular and transparent layers. She looks like an old Russian ballerina, hair pulled back, eyes sunken, green rings around them.

The blinking lights of the only illuminated piece, a kind of spider hanging above them in the air, give the party scene a menacing feel. The wrinkles on their faces appear and disappear. The spider's shadow falls across the rug in an intermittent and hungry manner.

Lucrecia is sitting in the background, at a table next to the telephone, waiting to be useful. She has the look of a soldier in the trenches awaiting the report. A marble lamp in the shape of a clitoris illuminates her body in warm tones.

Vilma falls asleep. The spider has stopped twinkling and seems ready to devour her. Poised right above her head.

Louise puts on music, the man slaps her ass. He pulls off her leotard. Positions her facedown, her belly sinking into the armchair. He draws a line up the line of her ass.

Lucrecia doesn't move. She looks away, but I can feel her rage. It pulsates. Then Vilma comes to and starts dancing or having a Parkinson's fit. I don't know what to make of that drooling skeleton embracing the others in a wild, electric dance. Spent or losing consciousness, the old woman lets her neck fall back and she collapses. Louise and her lover regard the old woman with disdain. It's Lucrecia who has to drag her onto the rug and cover her with her own jacket. Tragedy is a deformation of the absurd.

Space Disconnected

Lucrecia is cold and aloof in the morning. Before long, a look betrays her. She's acting. Her farce is exposed.

"I knew where to find you," she says to me.

"How?"

"You're different. You almost don't disgust me anymore."

"Thank you, how kind."

"Care to take a walk?"

"Are you kicking me out?"

"No, with me."

I don't know how to act with her. Default scorn is easiest. I look at her embarrassed and nod yes. Like a dog, I'm seduced. What's she plotting?

Out in the city, Lucrecia is actually spontaneous. It makes me feel clumsy.

We move away from the building on the pretext of hunger. Walk through the city center like tourists, adventuring. Our meandering brings us to the doors of the cathedral. I never went in before. Lucrecia encourages me to listen to a young girl giving a presentation in front of San Martín's tomb. Her reedy voice contrasts with the dramatic content it relates.

"The hero was buried head down. At a forty-five-degree

angle, pointed right at hell. Lack of space or revenge for his Freemasonry?"

For a moment, the student's words make me forget Lucrecia, who is already walking through the central nave.

"I need you."

The phrase hangs in front of me like a sock on a clothesline. If Lucrecia confesses, I'll bow down at her feet. But no. She's got something else on her mind.

"You have a weakness for what doesn't belong to you. Don't interrupt me. I have you on camera. I know what you took. And I don't judge you. Louise is a temptation."

"Why'd you bring me here?"

"Tomorrow I want you to quit."

"And what do I get?"

"Ask."

"A night with you."

"No."

"An hour together."

"Too much."

"Show me a tit."

"Come here. The confessional is empty."

A white light gives my sight an azure tint. She unbuttons her shirt. Lucrecia's skin stained in chiaroscuro, the moisture of the wood, her pointy nipples seem not of the same universe as the words that preceded them. I reach out a hand, into the abyss. The organ begins to sound from down below. I feel tiny, in ecstasy. She is *Saturnia pyri* with folded wings. Lucrecia's brown eyes glow false and expectant. We're enclosed alone, captive. And she, like a wild butterfly, lets me touch her.

"I'm not going anywhere," I say as I come.

She rips the hairpiece off my head. And drops it on the velvet bench. It looks like a rodent.

"You're obsessed with that man."

"Don't mess with him. And don't speak his name."

False Eye, Collage

I fall asleep and appear inside an insect collection. Run a finger through the viscous, translucent resin where multiple moths are trapped.

Now, the amber covers me completely, I'm naked and impregnated. I flap my arms in a contraction of fear. In the dream, Lucrecia watches me, with a pin between her fingers and blood-shot mouth. I am minuscule, like a *Stigmella ridiculosa*. A two-millimeter-long butterfly. Lucrecia smiles and pins me to the cork, next to photos of art installations. Like that, wings hardened, I'm nailed up in front of her like a dwarf Christ without mercy. I feel the pin like a dagger in my heart.

I wake up bathed in semen, thinking I love Lucrecia.

"Mother, forget the whole thing."

"What's that, my child?"

"I can't do it. I feel something new."

"You're just horny."

"No, Mother. This is important."

"Many fish in the sea. You'll find another."

"I can't. I want to do the right thing."

"We're so close, Severino."

"Think of me, Mother. Always alone and against my will."

"I'm with you."

"I don't want to ruin what's coming."

"Promise us that you'll forget Lucrecia. It's her, right?"

"I love her."

"But why? Love changes face, find someone real."

"You don't understand. It's her or no one."

"No, your love is your own. You invent it, you magnify it, get obsessed with it. Love is about the one who feels it. And you already have. You did. I love you very much. That harpy's not for you. She's the enemy."

"It's like a wild madness, what I feel. I've never felt it before, but it's growing. I hate her, Mother, so much I can't stop thinking about her."

"Listen to what you're saying. It's crazy."

"Like you. Look at your life."

"That's different. I'm already old. I want to die free, with a smile on my face."

"Don't talk like that."

"I deserve a little happiness. It's all in your hands. See you Saturday?"

I hang up, bewitched by the image of the pin. I want to find Lucrecia, grab her from behind, kiss the nape of her neck like a lukewarm worm. Bend her over something flat and fill with blood. But my past is a hindrance. The pathetic life is a powerful image that leaves no room for creation. The stigma of the absurd pricks like a thorn. Love doesn't eclipse, it sustains. It leaves no room for anything else, it's a question of volume. Spill the stagnant water. Only love will save us from the flood. Let the diving board not be destroyed before we jump.

But the poison of loneliness is never cured, its calling is eternity.

Setting the Stage

Now I lie still in the bedroom, living her body all over again. I
don't even know if it happened anymore. I don't trust happiness.
I'm used to suffering mental states, uncertain aches, emergen-
cies. I have a long list of irritations, voluptuous itching, maniacal dryness.

My hairpiece is gone. I go to the window and breathe in a
dose of the sharp hush night brings. It doesn't coincide in space
with my state of love newly ignited. But soon I feel a new kind
of power. My baldness makes me stronger. Never hide again.
Scarcity out in the open, like a banner.

Two soft knocks on the door bring me back to the present.
"Here I am."

Lucrecia enters and vanquishes me. We gorge ourselves, fill
our bodies with traces of the other. All at once, happiness no longer frightens me.

Portrait or Window

I can't take my eyes off the false head. I apply mascara to its lashes as a distraction, devote myself to imagining. I have strong ideas regarding what should happen. That's why it scares me that Severino is losing his way. He always falls over the edge. First the edge of the bed, then of everything else.

Then I lie down with the head beside me but don't sleep. I stay there, stretched out, looking up at the poorly painted ceiling, a faint green. A tear in the wallpaper, to one side of the closet, resembles the Colonel's face. If he saw the two of us looking up at him. She's the same, I'm not. I'm three times the age I was back then. But it's good to feel accompanied, to have a mental prosthesis accompany you. Two heads are better than one. But she's really slow. She needs help just to open and close her eyes. When she winks, it makes me laugh.

When the last train to Tigre passes, I fall asleep. I dream of a black robe that extends to my feet. I'm barefoot. Domingo, on his knees, kisses my toes. A true gentleman. When I wake up, the first thing I see is that the head is missing. It's fallen onto the floor.

It's like a pet. I take it all around the house. We eat breakfast together, we spray down the courtyard. If I have to go out, I leave her by the door. And I kiss her, so she'll bring me luck. I made her an altar by the doorway. I got rid of Severino's insect jars and put some dry flowers, a scented votive candle, a plaster angel, and a piece of green velvet in their place. A kind of refuge.

Contemplating her for a moment, praying to her, praying for my son, speaking through her in a direct line to the eternal, makes me feel connected. And good.

Suddenly, an urge to end it all. End times, take the train to Retiro, go inside, destroy the paintings, watch blood flow like a dark river. But no, be brave. Hold avarice in check, control it. Water down my animality with a cup of tea. The first time I saw Louise was on the cover of *Siete Días*. On the arm of the Colonel. What excitement when we saw the ad. Butler needed for Service Work, Organizing, and Cleaning. Required: familiarity with Art and the ability to stay overnight from Monday to . . . , her name, at the end of all of that, was huge.

I phone Severino to keep from thinking, to pass my malaise off on him.

"Why didn't you come?" My voice sounds ugly.

"They changed my day off."

"It's been a week since I've heard anything from you. Tell me the truth."

"There's nothing to tell. Everything is in motion."

"Don't forget the pain. It's an overgrown plant."

"I'm aware."

"Still in love or have you come back? Remember that madness and desire drink from the same bottle."

"All better now."

"Oh, I'm glad."

Color Techniques. Fiend

"We're off to Berlin. The Mauer has come down. Help Lucrecia with the bags."

"What came down?"

"The Wall, my dear. Read a newspaper, please."

"In the city center?"

"What world are you living in? Stay here while we're gone. I'll pay you later."

"How many days?"

"However many it takes. I want an open space in the living room and some barbed wire. But no rush. They're keeping the best pieces. Lucrecia, do you have the money?"

Lucrecia is dragging two huge designer suitcases. They're both wearing hats. Louise's is ridiculous, capeline style.

"I'm going down. Apprise Severino of the security protocols."

Once the mistress is gone, I try to kiss Lucrecia.

"If you take anything, I'm turning you in. Don't ever touch me again. Forget it. It was a moment of weakness. I'm back with Manfredo."

She closes the elevator door in my face and I'm alone. My

hands are moist. Manfredo. The sound of that name turns my stomach. I walk in circles around the kitchen. A rush of nerves makes the pounding of my heart reverberate like a bell. I want to smoke but don't know how. I prowl like a wolf in the night. I go to Lucrecia's room. I throw myself down on the bed. Rub my face against her sheets, like one possessed. The bare portion of the mattress looks like a wound. I sit to keep from falling. The discomfiture exits my stomach and curls up beside me. I stand. I hate that man. I hate him with unknown intensity.

I move through the apartment without feeling my legs. I want to scream, but moan instead. The front door is closed, everything the same as always. Absolute emptiness. Veins at a standstill, a kind of vertigo in my face. I throw myself down on the floor in the living room and stay there for a while, like a puddle you have to jump over.

The telephone interrupts one terror, generating another.

"How's everything?" she says coldly.

"Mother!"

"What's wrong? Have you been drinking?"

"No, I just got up."

"Don't waste time, find the safe, do something. It's now or never, react. I'm already old, we've got a narrow window of opportunity."

The call is cut off. An aqueous sound floods my eardrum. I hang up. I'm breathing heavily, like a swimmer coming out of the ocean. The phone rings again.

"Mother, I have to stay here for an indefinite period of time."

"What happened? Are you losing it?"

"No. Send a *Loxosceles* with Augusto."

"A what?"

"You know the insect jars I have in the cupboard by the sink? Send me the one that has the green perforated top."

"What for?"

"Nothing in particular. I want to show it to someone, that's all."

"Think of us, Severino."

"That's what I'm doing. Send it."

"Don't hurt anybody."

"Mother, who do you think I am?"

Worse for Everyone

Severino shuts himself in and I call the pharmacist's son. The boy has to figure out how to clear his head. His mind is a trap full of drawers. Open and remove, polish clean. Gnaw a few words.

He told me sad things: the qualities of a work of art are its defects. Severino thinks he's somebody, a future contemporary artist. Poor boy. He's got a potpourri. We're all works of art in the process of decay. His voice sounded childish and he hung up on me.

Alas. I sent the wrong jar. The one with the black top.

Worse for everyone.

She Gets Lost

I open the jar and the spider slips out between Lucrecia's sheets. I shut the door. Mother was right, I repeat to myself. Love's an invention. Each of us generates our own sickness. I pour myself some coffee and change my mind. The word love sends me flying back to her. Lucrecia's little ass and the *Loxosceles laeta* must not coincide in time. The spider hides a personal project of mine and should be put back in her jar. Who could explain it: now yes, now no. Intractable fear. Don't touch her. Don't look at her. Her six eyes will fix on Lucrecia. Multiplied she'll be more appetizing.

I put on gloves and go to the bedroom to find the spider. She's not there. She's not there? I slip my fingers like tentacles into corners. I look like a lunatic, like a drug dog at the airport. I flip the mattress in disbelief. I shake the sheets to make her fall out, to show herself. The cunning little creature assumes the color of what surrounds her. She's gone. Not even a trace of web. I look desperately everywhere. I lift clothes off the floor, pick up some panties. NOTHING. I shut the door.

I walk to the store with my body and remain with Lucrecia and the spider in my mind. I'm split in two; I'm pathetic. I need

to breathe, but the city is a stifling stomach. People hurry, flee-
ing the heat.

In the store, there's a ceiling fan and layer of grease on the
display racks. I go to the aerosol sprays, hypnotized by a bumblebee zigzagging above a box of grapes. The beauty of that dance
contrasts with the banality of the human faces. People are too
mammalian. Swine waiting around for the end. I spray a little poison at the bee, but no. It's for spiders, it doesn't work on
anthophiles. Death is excessively specific. I get in line and want
to scream: the grave awaits! Hurry up. The people in front of me
seem less like people and more like cutouts. Vacant, plaster casts.

I run back. Call the elevator. Arriving on the fourteenth
floor, I feel a vague anxiety. Is it just me or does it smell like
something's burning?

Fuck the Wall, Graffiti

Manfredo and Vilma Cohen are smoking in the living room, they look like actors from an old film. He's got on a linen suit. She, an A-line dress covered in faded flowers, a necklace dangling to her navel, and a purse slung over one shoulder. Even though she's sitting down. A lazy cloud floats above them.

"How'd you get in?" I say, poorly masking my fury.

"The door," a laugh followed by a fit of coughing bursts from the old woman's lips.

"We came to celebrate. Will you bring us bourbon?" Manfredo makes a hideous sound in his throat.

"What're you celebrating?" I ask.

"Louise got her hands on a gorgeous two-and-a-half-ton block. *Fuck the wall.* And graffiti with two men kissing each other on the mouth. Great, right?" Vilma seems the most festive.

"Yeah, great. And they're bringing it back?" I sit.

"They're going to phone in half an hour. So we'll all be together," *Señora* Cohen says, catching her breath.

"Don't forget that bourbon, kid. What're you drinking, Vilma?"

"Champagne, of course."

In the kitchen, I curse silently. Motherfucker. When I return with the drinks, Manfredo is lying on the glass divan. He's naked and nobody cares. What's more, Vilma is touching his feet, distractedly, like someone stroking a hamster. I imagine him from underneath. Ass plastered against the glass, a temptation of blood that can't be tasted. His cock is massive, even flaccid. Why show it?

"Apparently they were asking a fortune, but came down after a while," *Señora* Cohen states enigmatically.

"Some friends are handling the Mauer affair. Because you have to get it here too," Manfredo responds self-importantly.

"Imagine that," Vilma says, not really getting it.

"Train to Hamburg, boat to Buenos Aires, customs. That's where I come in."

"Ah, so she's not bringing it now?" Vilma asks, uncorking the bottle.

"Getting it here takes . . ."

"And where's she going to put it?"

"A mystery. But I can store it for her in a warehouse. I brought the photographs, my dear. They came."

"The German ones?"

"Apparently the whore was a Social Democrat and a candidate."

"Like you!" Vilma and Manfredo bust out laughing.

"I think they're fake," I say. "That sword is from here."

"What do you mean, from here?" Manfredo gives me a scathing look.

"Argentine military."

"Can't be. A cultured butler. How extravagant. So they don't cost a fortune? Run along, my dear, don't stand there like a nail. Go do your duties," Manfredo shoos me away and I go, with a false smile.

"I love all of them,"Vilma is shouting. "*Pour le liberté!*"

"*La liberté,*" Manfredo corrects her, arching an eyebrow.

"Whatever . . . I'll give you the check tomorrow."

"Cash, my love."

"They're divine, I'll cherish them."

Their giggles seem like dull darts, they drop to the rug. I watch them from the studio. I hope Loxosceles kills them both. She could be anywhere. Her venom pulsates in the presence of strangers. In the living room, two *hymenopterans*. With the zoom, I survey their surroundings, searching for the spider. Impossible image of death as defense. The two of them stretched out on the living-room floor, covered in blisters. Sobs, cries for help.

But the arachnid doesn't appear and now in the living room they dance. Manfredo appears to sing while clapping arrhythmically. Stupidity and tedium arouse his soul.

Vilma gets dizzy and Manfredo saves her from cracking her head on the coffee table. I resist the party's routine. The phone rings and Manfredo dives on the device like someone awaiting a medical report. Seeing him so generous, shamelessly displaying his member, undermines his sincerity.

Suddenly, reality happens in the living room. Vilma falls to one side with the photos in hand. Nobody breaks her fall. Manfredo keeps talking to Berlin and doesn't even register the moment *Señora* Cohen strikes her forehead against a glass skull a meter in diameter. The old woman lets slip a feeble moan and her blood stains the piece. She loses consciousness, if she ever had it. Manfredo hears the blow and shrieks, Severino!

When I enter the living room, anguish balloons in me like a wild mushroom. I don't want to touch that body, to clean that stain. The photographs leave me frozen. That obscenity out in the open. Absurd images where Mother is kissed by a wooden android, while a deformed boy forces himself into her. There's no doubt it's her, her face is repeated with sepia clarity in every photograph. Others, slightly sulfated.

Manfredo calls for Cotton, Forceps, Rubbing Alcohol, Band-Aids, while continuing to talk to Louise on the phone.

"Do it yourself. It grosses me out."

"Lou, my dear, I must go. Let's talk later. I have to attend to a matter of some delicacy."

A demonic look stops his breath for an instant.

"Get Cotton and pour a little Alcohol on it, sanitize the Forceps and then see if you can remove the Little Piece of Glass that I can see from here, above her Eyebrow. Clean the Wound and put a Band-Aid on it."

"Nurse I am not," I respond with conviction. "If you can't deal with it, let's call an ambulance. The number is by the phone."

"You're playing the part, my dear."

My own backbone surprises me. I walk out without answering, destination unknown. Manfredo comes up behind me and grabs me by my pants. With one hand he squeezes my throat. I feel his other fist against my ass.

"Don't fuck with me or I'll make you my *señorita*."

I'm paralyzed. I feel a slight erection.

Bravura

"Louise, my dear. Vilma got three stitches. It could've been worse. Your employee is heartless and not supportive at all. He left me to deal with the problem on my own. Can you believe it?"

Manfredo's voice on the telephone is like a meat grinder. Words breaking off from lack of intelligence. He sings his song with one hand on his chest. Vilma is sleeping in the guest room and there she'll stay. The combination of the festivities and the injury was more than enough to knock her out.

I feel bad. I don't know what to do. I sit in silence.

The ashtrays are full of roaches, and there's a green stain on the table.

"Luckily the cut was superficial. The skull cracked, but it's incredible how well it stood up to the blow. Almost intact. You've got it insured, right?"

Manfredo hangs up and comes toward me, not making eye contact.

"Okay, I'm going. Let Vilma sleep as long as she wants. If possible, offer her something to eat. If possible. *Nobody* forces *Anybody* to do *Anything* here."

Manfredo puts the erotic photographs in his pocket and walks out. But he forgot one under the table. When the elevator closes, I take it. I rescue Mother from the claws of that crow.

Garden of Eden, Detail

Vilma is still sleeping. Two days have passed and she remains in the same absent state. This morning, it seemed odd that she would still be silent. I went to check on her and she was in the same position we left her in after the fall. She's breathing, but unresponsive.

I get a glass of cold water and pour it over her head. She looks like a whitefish or a sleeping beauty sans dwarfs. And nobody to kiss her. She doesn't wake up.

I change the sweaty sheets in a state of revulsion. I set Vilma down on the floor, because I don't know where else to put her. I move her without effort. She weighs nothing. Like a cardboard woman, like the ones I stack up in my dreams. I consider picking her up with one hand, folding her, and leaving her outside so the doorman will take her away with the trash. But I put her back on the bed. I ponder the accident, I call Mother, I tell her.

"Look at *Señora* Cohen without blinking, for twenty seconds. There, right there. Focus on her face for me."

The image reaches Mother, with a few black spots.

"She's in a coma. She's dreaming. She sees herself young and happy, at a picnic or something. There are birds, a fountain, a dark lake. One man naked, another dressed. But I can't see them clearly. She's blonde and her hair is long."

"Should I call Louise?"

"I don't think she's coming back."

"Yes, wait, what do you mean not coming back?"

"No, I mean Vilma. She's in her image of Heaven. Even if she's dumb as a doornail, she won't be back. Here she's cadaverous and alone. There, a man is about to rub her down with oil. You okay?"

"I can't."

Image 8: Balm

The door to the elevator opens and a very flustered Manfredo enters. He's accompanied by a gaunt doctor: one Umpiérrez. He walks to the middle of the room and claps his hands together to summon me. The upper class effaces the identity markers of others. They never remember names.

"Someone!"

He counts to three and, when nobody appears, gestures to the doctor. They go behind the mirror door.

"Vilma, I brought the best specialist in all of Buenos Aires. Doctor, she's all yours."

"Relax and leave me alone with her," the doctor says in a milky voice. Spittle pooling in the corners of his mouth.

"Yes, good. I need a drink."

Manfredo leaves the room and runs into me in the hallway.

"Is everyone deaf here? Where's the guy who cleans?"

"That's me."

"Can you make coffee or are you just eye candy?"

He sits in the living room until the doctor comes back with a curious expression. He licks his lips a couple times and then advances through sentences with the density of oil.

"The *señora* is in a state of deep unconsciousness, caused by her recent trauma. She has damage to the right frontal lobe, a weak pulse, and ocular dryness."

"Yes, Doctor, but the wound was properly treated."

"I wouldn't rule out some other incident. Has she taken an opiate?"

"Not that I know of," Manfredo interjects.

"I observe a placebo happiness. Excess optimism: let me explain. Opium, also called poppy, produces happy somnolence, increases tactile sensations, causes tingling and itching. The *señora* has all the symptoms, but, in addition, she knows she's dreaming. She has good control of the back brain. She's manipulating images and is surprisingly active in the face of nothingness. Her dreams have an erotic bent, excessively so for a woman of her age. Her panties are wet."

"How interesting," Manfredo lies. "So pleasure is only for the young? You even deny fantasy."

"No, please: let me explain. Could I get a little gin? My mouth is dry."

"Yes, of course. Help yourself."

"Your coffee," I say, holding out the cup.

"Silence, please! Doctor Umpiérrez is talking," Manfredo interrupts, shouting.

"Relax, Manfredo. You're not doing your prostate any good. I said that the *señora's* overall condition is positive, apart from the coma and the hypertension. But I think it's good she's expressing her sexual instincts. Her head is hers. You know me, I've resolved more complex cases. Vilma is a breeze compared to the disorders I've had to deal with. Don't get me started on your operations, Manfredito."

"When I grow up I want to be just like you, Umpiérrez," Manfredo jokes. Nobody laughs.

I arrange catalogues, deciding to stay in the living room.

"Is it up to you what's to be done with her?" the doctor asks.

"We have to wait for Louise to come home. *Señora* Cohen has no family," with revulsion, the beast Manfredo reassumes control.

"Ah, one small thing, given the current picture. I did notice a peculiar bitemark on her lower abdomen."

"What kind of bitemark?" I interject.

"A bug bite of some kind. Nothing serious. The bite happened less than ten minutes ago. A little topical ice and a balm will leave her right as rain. Coincidentally, I have a sample with me."

I move quickly and take the balm. Practically tearing it from the hands of the doctor, who has accumulated enough drool to make a soup.

"Allow me."

"By all means," Umpiérrez says, surprised. "What a solicitous fellow."

I go with long strides to the guest room, leaving the others behind. When I lift her gown, I recognize the symptoms. The flesh is already darkening.

"Loxosceles bit her."

I unmake the bed, searching for her. I sniff around in every corner. The initial terror turns into laughter. Something about the pathetic order of things. I leave no corner unchecked, as a cackling seizes my throat. A combination of nerves and hysterical shock that sounds like repressed mania.

When I open the closet, everything changes. Built into the wall, a safe. I'm stunned. I almost faint.

Without a sound, I put the closet as it was and adjust to the disaster. I no longer consider the danger. The sky has opened up. Revealing the source of happiness.

Deaf Ears, Tableau

After he delivers the news, I dictate a number to Severino, we'll see if it's right: 1633081991803361.

I kneel before the false head and light two candles. Eyes half closed and hair pulled back off my forehead. My neck bending, as if it were a separate body, a different animal.

"I'm not worthy."

I remain in a state of near ecstasy, breathing in time with the boy. Deep and slightly ragged exhalations. My nostrils inhale the air of Victoria and flare with a vague pleasure: a soft tickle, a lick of the spiritual.

"Let him do the right thing. Let grace guide him."

Lana's head makes conversation possible amid all this silence. Only the train can cut off a phrase. The clamor of its passing punctuates the infinite cries for help, memories, or ideas for the future that roll off my tongue. I'm ready for change.

"The glory of the future: what could be. Present and past are a crushing baseness. What couldn't be, can't be. What's to come is wholesome ambition. We've already had misery. We cultivate the future. Let the spirit drive us toward what's yet to come."

Lana is unaffected, she remains fixed in her immobility, with typical android stubbornness. Though beautiful, she's hard.

"Dear Colonel. Stay where you are, soon our souls will merge. Don't stray far from this first world, wait for me in the second. Beyond that, souls accelerate and are united with the celestial ovum. Once there, you won't be recognizable. The ovum equalizes. Confounds."

I remember your death. I brought flowers to your grave and stood off to one side. How I wept. You were a gentleman, despite everything. Nobody came to say goodbye. You were alone. In the coffin, I asked them to bury you with a piece of your creation. You never got to be happy with Lana. Maybe in the Hereafter. But they didn't allow it. The people from the funeral home pushed me away. Remember? No, how could you remember if you were no longer there. For a while, I got to play the android-object of your affections. Because she was out of commission, not even half her circuitry in working order. I had to imitate her. I was the copy of the copy of the copy. And I lifted my legs, flexed them back so that they seemed even firmer than hers.

How grateful I was when you gave me this piece of Lana. Her sad little head. I confess that it saved me from loneliness. We even bathe together sometimes. Bah, I bathe and she sits on top of the toilet, watching me.

"Domingo, give me light. Don't leave us in this darkness of reason that hurts so much. Let our eyes be purer. Oh, and if it's not too much to ask, get me away from the train tracks. I want an apartment in the city center. If you can. Amen."

Orgasmic Piety, Freehand

Final minutes of baseness. A glass stairway will lead me to freedom. The contents of the safe will save my life from the lack of color. Perched astride good fortune, I'll greet everyone as an equal.

Manfredo is getting ready to go out. Louise asked him to stay in the house until she got back. But an event will keep him occupied until quite late. When at last he leaves, I walk to the guest room. Turn on the light. Vilma remains in her oneiric rigidity. I move about as if I were alone. I open the closet. A leg leaves a groove in the pine boards. Vilma's breathing changes. She lets out a kind of anguished moan. I look at her. I approach.

Señora Cohen smiles. A tremor seizes her body. She licks her lips, thirsty. A sudden fever is making her hair stand on end. I recognize the symptoms. The venom is spreading, celebrating the possession of her arteries.

All of a sudden, as if in a trance, she looks up at me.

"Kiss me, please. I'm dying."

Without a word, my eyes wet, I do as she asks. I feel moved by a fatalistic piety. My lips touch hers. They're hot. Like kissing a swamp. The old woman puts her tongue in my mouth and slowly toys with my palate. That dense eel makes it hard to breathe. But I let the viscous creature have control. She grips my neck, her dry, pointy fingernails dig into my flesh. Her rank claws ensnare me.

I feel suffused with her, sucked to the bone, when Vilma releases a soft shriek, inside, as if something were pulling a little harder. A faint tremor in her pubic region announces the denouement. She is gone.

I expected an orgasm and instead I'm prisoner of a dead woman. I can't get her hands off my neck. I end up ripping them away with fury. Vilma is all dried out, her face sated. It had been a long time since she'd kissed anybody. Years.

A sound in the living room brings me back to reality. It sounds like Lucrecia's voice. I shut the closet and turn off the light. I walk out.

"She's gone," I say, without greeting her.

"What? I just got here, make me tea."

"Vilma is dead."

"Don't refer to her so informally."

Lucrecia leaves me and walks decisively to the guest room. She turns on the light. A scream. I go to her. She's frozen.

"What happened? Haven't you ever seen a dead body?"

She can't answer. She looks at me, her pupils dilated.

"Calm down, Lucrecia," I take her into the bathroom. I splash water on her wrists.

"A spider," she says, looking in the mirror.

"Where?" I jump.

"In Vilma's mouth," Lucrecia starts to shake, hysterical. "That disgusting thing was in her mouth. As if it had come out from inside! Huge and dark, covered with eyes. It looked at me!"

Lucrecia loses it, rinses out her mouth, brushes her teeth,

shakes out her clothes, pushes me out, and shuts herself in. I grab an exceedingly heavy book on Pop Art and go, ready to finish off the spider.

When I get back to Vilma's bed, Loxosceles is gone. But with white thread she has sealed the dead woman's lips.

Fatal Aesthetic

Once she gets over her bout of disgust, Lucrecia gets swept up in the event, testing out her aesthetic vision of the fates. Body, woe, music, degustation, suffering, cremation: last words. Pain is a precious moment. The death invites her to lose her mind. A magnificent abracadabra fixes the quotidian with its patina of gravity. Life without death is shrunken, vulgarized. Almost not worth living. The sum of meaningless moments is resolved by the denouement. The exactitude of the calculation exalts.

The mortuary cosmetologist arrives early and sets up next to *Señora* Cohen with her dirty and rank little valise. It's tricky work. Vilma's body is breaking down by the second. A layer of wax would be more effective than any base. Her eyes are so sunken that nobody can find them. Black Parisian sunglasses save her from looking like an electrical outlet. Her skin is a delicate lie without bone to support it. Nothing under her cheekbones but wasted years and the accretion of crushing tedium, all of which tends to melt away without the tautness of life. Her nose looks like a nail, weak and bent. Poorly pounded into the middle of her face. Vilma was held together by a thread. If she hadn't died, she would've gone to pieces.

Waiting her turn, the hairstylist reads a novel. Every so often she looks up and arches an eyebrow. Finally, she occupies the seat at the head of the table and pulls a thick, miraculously natural weave out of her bag, because a wig would be impossible. Nobody will notice the gap. Fortunately, her nape won't be visible, because of the angle of her body. But the reddish hue contrasts starkly with the rest of the corpse. All that's left of Vilma are crumbs of humanity. The off-white of badly washed pottery. She looks like the yellowed page of a book. A false- and fierce-looking image. The intrusion of that hair makes her look even deader.

The mortician selects an old little pink dress, characteristic of women of means of a certain age. A nearby jeweler lends a double string of cultured pearls, on the condition that his name be mentioned discreetly during the wake. But oh how difficult it is to put clothes on a broomstick. Her extreme thinness upsets the mortician. Not even the smallest size fits right around the model, so stiff, so otherworldly. She starts with nylon stockings and ends up distraught. Why does she spend her time doing such inhuman work? The dead woman's cold feet, her dry and chipped nails are revolting. The nylon catches on the big toe of her right foot and the stockings tear, an interminable run all the way to her thigh. The second pair gets tangled at the knees. Twisted. She decides to doctor the length of the skirt to keep the tangle out of sight. Vilma lengthens, loses form. But nobody will notice. Only me. The sadness of the mourners will keep them from perceiving the absurdity. Death makes a mockery of objectivity.

Her lip color is cause for controversy, heatedly debated. Who will apply the finishing touch? The mortician maintains that it's her responsibility. The hairdresser—against all odds—supports her. The tone of the discussion escalates and Lucrecia intervenes.

"A refined lady cannot go to the afterlife in bright colors. It looks cheap. Lips, same color as the dress. She'll be bright on the inside."

The red cushions they used for another dead woman won't work on this occasion. But an elegant silk shop offers to donate five meters of ivory brocade and an onsite seamstress, in exchange for *Señora* Cohen's debts being settled. A designer sketches the deathbed. A double row of roses, orchids, and lilies at the head, a lisianthus flower in her hands, and a simple row of pampas grass at her feet, for a wild and autochthonous touch.

A well-known performer would play Vilma's favorite piece: Viola (Solo) Sonata, op. 25, no. 1, fourth movement, by Hindemith. The speed of the piece would oblige him to remain standing. To avoid inconveniencing the mourners, the musician would move around without stopping anywhere. Hindemith is very reiterative.

The invitations are sent out right away and the garlands start arriving almost instantly. They are positioned strategically, by size. The building fills with the smell of a freshly watered garden. The olfactory bloom gives me vertigo. Everyone's nostrils flare, tickle. The glut of aromatic bliss is a tragedy for the senses. From the nose to the silence.

At one thirty, the catering is ready. The waitresses, in strict mourning, move around with red and black caviar on trays of white gold. Lucrecia doesn't want the refreshments to cause more olfactory chaos amongst the guests. Death should be as odorless as possible. Nothing sadder than a malodorous funeral.

Apparently Louise will arrive around two. She stopped off in Paris, to buy herself a Dior, befitting the tragedy. Even in the worst moments she thinks of herself. Of how she'll look.

Vilma Has Departed, Speech

What do we think of death? Horror. The line separating reality from the beyond. Death brings down all bodies.

How do you say goodbye to a friend without pondering your own departure?

With Vilma, a piece of me goes too. And no more than that, because I have to go on. Vilma was a mentor: a born collector, acute and passionate. Capable of giving up love to purchase the right piece. Art controlled her body like a maniacal king controls his rabble. Vilma did so much for the local scene. She brought in unknown work. Held New York up before our wild eyes.

Who ever imagined she would leave us so unexpectedly? Everyone. She made her departure with that same decisiveness as always. Without awaiting approval.

Where else could her ashes come to rest but in the Tate? All of you will travel with me. James Packard will do a show with her remains. A body in the ground, a reconstruction of Vilma's silhouette. Art against Death, the great battle. James's index finger will sketch the collector. To one side, the audience will remove their shoes. We'll walk barefoot across her. *Make love with your feet*: We'll bury her.

What do we think of death? Nothing. There's no possible idea for which it isn't important. The world ends here, at the level of the heart. The rest is pure verse.

Why weep, if subtlety exists.

Break out the champagne. Applaud *Señora* Cohen and never forget her name.

Vilma, Vilma, Vilma.

The guests enter into an unexpected ecstasy, moved by Louise's rhetoric. Her eloquence has freed them from thinking. The Hindemith sonata lets loose the madness. Some jump, others slip and spill alcohol on the rugs without meaning to. A torrent of lips collides with the hard cheek of the hostess, accustomed to adeptly burying all comers.

Lucrecia clinks glasses with her mistress and her tear ducts glisten. She cannot hide her unconditional admiration.

Manfredo raises his glass from the opposite side of the living room and later finds Louise's mouth and kisses it in an insolent gesture.

She pushes him away with indifference.

"Not now, dear. There are people here."

I want it all to end. I've had too much to drink and my criminal eyes are impossible to hide. A burning desire to cut the throat of the first person who crosses my path seizes my hands. But laughter absorbs my entire skeleton. I can't hide the sensation of hilarity that these things produce in me.

Vilma's friends seem exultant, snorting cocaine off every sideboard, maybe they'll return to her later. Pale and abstracted from the revelry, the old woman sinks deeper into the bed. Only a fraction of her face is still visible. The mattress will swallow her and nobody will notice.

I take advantage of all the activity to leave a belated gift: the tape of Lucrecia and Manfredo under Louise's pillow.

Senza Pietà, Detail

In the morning, I get up early, drink a maté, and go to the cemetery. I want to see the burial with my own eyes. Fifty black cars compose a dark line. The corpse leads the procession, crowned with flowers.

They arrive at Recoleta under a divine rain. The weather scowls at the mourners. There won't be any speeches apparently. A pervasive unease hinders a good turn of phrase.

The rain changes its mind and decides to inundate every tomb, every shoe. The guests run to the crematory and wait there for the coffin to arrive. The ground is slippery and the workers walk slowly, looking at their feet. I hide behind the black veil of the woman in front of me. I'm unsettled. The elegance of the mourning makes me uncomfortable. I should've worn shoes and not these rubber boots.

A mobile countertop draws Vilma's coffin up to the sliding door through which it will disappear. Nobody has the nerve to touch her. A few inaudible phrases are chewed up and at last the little door opens and she passes into the infernos of a refractory oven. To tell the truth, the moment is beautiful. I'm one of the lucky ones, up in the second row.

As I'm about to leave, the finale has an unexpected complication. A sudden explosion prompts thoughts of an attack. Then, a furious functionary appears.

"Did the *señora* use a pacemaker?" he asks with a face of revulsion.

"No idea, why?" *Señora* Louise answers.

"You need to get that information before having a friend cremated. Something exploded, and now the furnace's retort has been damaged."

"What?"

"You're going to have to wait a while. Her body blew apart. The ceiling of the oven cracked. The only thing of use is the skull. Would you like us to crush that so you can take it now, or do you want to have a coffee, wait a little while, and see if we find something more?"

"Oh, I don't know, what a mess. Manfredo, what do you think?"

"Give us the skull and ciao. We're not about to spend eternity waiting around here."

"Either way you're going to have to pay a fine for the explosion."

"Can I write a check? I didn't bring cash."

"This way."

The marble urn is nearly empty. Better not to think of what's missing. Powerful people reduced to so little.

I return to Victoria, happy. I like cemeteries. Besides, it's been a long time since I went to the city center. I tell Lana everything. She almost smiles.

Pause

I take advantage of the burial to finish the job. I plug in the shorted electric razor and the circuit trips immediately. The alarm starts to make the intermittent beeping of a canary in a coal mine: pi pi pi. The cameras stop recording. A pale light enters through the half-open windows.

The room where Vilma was still smells. When I open the window, Buenos Aires invades me with its rigid madness. Ambulances intertwine tongues in orgasmic wailing.

I open the door to the closet and dial the numbers into the safe.

16 33 08 19 91 80 33 61

But I don't open it. An apparition stops me short: the disappeared spider has descended from the ceiling and hangs before my eyes, regarding me, sinister. The end projected by the multiple pupils disarms me, leaves me useless. A few centimeters is all that separates my nose from that invitation to the end of my world. Should I run? Smash it with my head? I don't move.

She enjoys this. She knows the terror she provokes. And she takes advantage of the paralysis of her enemy, executing an unexpected maneuver: she swings up into my left nostril. Swift little warrior.

The world loses interest, automatically. Everything is reduced to a nasal cavity. I start to blow, desperate. I cover the right orifice, stick a finger into the left, cough, spit. All at once. No luck. An attempt at heavy gargling fails to stop her. She advances into that damp cave, sashays into the closed circuit of my respiration, with the assurance of a quadrille.

I go to the bathroom, like Lucrecia before me. I attempt to drown the intruder, filling my nose with water. But the eight legs traipse capriciously through my pharynx. They successfully pass the epiglottis, reaching the larynx, pausing to rest for a moment in that moisture. In the trachea, she's lost. Sensation of drowning. Death is a repulsive sensation. I look at myself in the mirror and all I see is a man condemned, the wet and shining eyes of one awaiting the shot. The venom seeks a nest in my lung. Each breath could be my last. I'm afraid to obstruct the spider with my exhalations.

The vice of existence evaporates in front of that safe. I touch it like an engorged vulva. But it won't open. So, I go to the window, lean half my body out into the rain. I'm going to fall.

But the spider speaks in my ear with a sticky whisper: *Don't even think of jumping. You live for me.*

I shut the window, obedient. I put the closet in order. I run my fingertips down my neck, mirroring death's trajectory. Loxosceles advances beyond my palate and continues down, powerful, to its dark hiding place.

An invisible grimace grips the corners of my lips and fixes them to the edge of my face. Like a bird on a sheet of Styrofoam.

Victoria, Chinese Ink

I buy a ticket. One way. I have to repeat the destination twice. The word Victoria gets lost in the back of my throat. The spider has robbed me of all certainty. When I reach the platform, I don't have the nerve even to sit.

I feel her circulating. Moving through me. Lurking in soft spaces, seeking the perfect location. Somewhere warm and dark to spin her web.

I board the train with the spider on alert. But I take certain pleasure in denial. Her or me. *You'll be my vessel, my environs. Who is the parasite?* I enter the last car, almost on tiptoe. I dodge people to keep from upsetting her. I'm afraid of accelerating my death. Of not making it home.

The train advances and I am frozen with terror. An urge to throw myself out the poorly latched door. But my body doesn't react. She puts my arms to sleep. She takes charge of everything. If I look, she's there, in my eyes. A slight itch on the nape of my neck, her. And yet, Loxosceles bides her time. Silent, a wise creature that knows what it wants.

I wait for the sudden and penetrating bite in the dome of my diaphragm to leave me breathless. But my death is postponed. It's capable of not manifesting. I start an arachnoid conversation with the sleuth, which feels like a furious monologue. I hiss, subdued by horror. Just a few awful phrases of idiotic promise. Anything to live. Crooked attempts to curry her favor. Loxosceles ignores me, tracing and retracing my anatomy like a medical examiner. But she feels less vital.

The awareness of my death ends up fortifying me. I've passed from horror to certainty: I'm mortal, it's just that simple. I'll die with or without her.

I find a position in the seat that makes me feel safe: hunched up facing the wall, my eyes at a forty-five-degree angle. My breathing deepens and I say to myself that I'll avoid death through proper inhalation. Maybe I'll pull her up into my mouth, spit her out.

The Same Dull Object

The block of the Mauer sets sail for Buenos Aires while in the courtyard Mother bites an apple. The sound of the front door pulls her out of her lazy mastication.

"Severino, is that you? We have a visitor."

"It's over, Mother."

"Good afternoon," Manfredo comes out of the bathroom with wet hands.

"This is an old friend. Bah, the son of an old friend."

The 11:15 Retiro train vibrates the windows.

"I found a photograph that belongs to me in your suitcase. Look," Manfredo puts on glasses.

"How odd!" I stammer.

"And we were saying how this whore looks a lot like your mother."

"Yes, a bit."

"A kind of copy. I'm shorter. And dignified."

"Yes, of course," Manfredo chuckles.

Mother dissembles, offended by herself. There's nothing I can say.

"We're the measure of external horror. We surrender our bodies to the violence of the other," he seems to be citing me, he's read my notebook.

I feel bitterness in my alveoli. A dark stain.

"Why are you here?" I snap.

"Your mother is going to have to move, my dear."

"Is that right?" the spider helps me.

"And soon. The estate finally came through. Many years have passed. This house belonged to my father."

"The Colonel said it was mine," Mother is sad.

"What are you talking about?"

Manfredo is silent for a moment and then Mother starts to remember like a sleepwalker. The past presents itself with unforeseen violence.

"It was a national holiday, I don't remember which one. There were rosettes everywhere. The Colonel wanted an *interesting* photo. That's what Lana said."

"Don't be ridiculous, *Señora*. Be discreet."

"Naked from the waist up, you blindfolded me on the rooftop. You gave me instructions and an LP. Like in a movie I didn't see, I was nobody. You dressed me up to torture Aurora."

"What're you talking about, shut up," Manfredo is nervous.

"The wind gave me vertigo but it was my last responsibility. I bent my back, contracted my ribs. A foolish excitement filled my mouth. Reality never interested me. My nipples were hard, my hair pulled back. I threw the disc, but never heard the camera's click."

"Where's the deed?" Manfredo rummages through the credenza, the shelves.

"When I came down, there were some screams. But I'd been given money and an order: don't look back, don't turn around. I obeyed."

"What's this doing here?" Manfredo reels back when he

242

discovers Lana's head, which looks back at him, ringed by candles and scented smoke.

"Who killed your mother? Was it me? Tell me the truth."

"Enough, you sow. Shut your mouth," Manfredo wraps his hands around Mother's throat.

Loxosceles can't take it anymore and tells me to grab him by the hair. To bite his mouth. *Seize the moment.*

Manfredo didn't have time to react. He ended up stretched out on the floor. It took Mother a while to come to, which gave me time to dig a hole in the courtyard.

It was dark. The spider was asleep. Mother wept until the snoring took her. I didn't sleep a wink that night. I left early.

Without Light There Is No Form

When I get back to Retiro, Louise has already showered and is giving orders with renewed energy. Lucrecia assigns me tasks in the archives.

At lunch, the triangle converges and comes full circle. The private incidents are absorbed with studied indifference.

Nobody will betray that imitation of naturalness. Louise has disconnected the VCR. And won't bring it up. She'd rather have Lucrecia and me live in discomfort, hemmed in by the illusion of the cameras. Discontent is the greatest guarantee of progress.

Did she watch the tape?

Before dinner, I go down to the street without explanation. The proximity of death makes me behave differently. Turning toward the river, a kind of beautiful spirituality enters my soul. Something is soothed: the discontent of being alive and not knowing why. But that doubt accompanies every being who crosses my path. Death equalizes and disorients. Whose body is this, whose voice? Loxosceles is my mistress.

I decide not to go on. To give my interior life to her.

Aurora (Canción a la Bandera)

Alta en el cielo un águila guerrera,
Audaz se eleva al vuelo triunfal,
Azul un ala del color del cielo,
Azul un ala del color del mar.

Es la bandera de la patria mía,
Del sol nacida que me ha dado Dios;
Es la bandera de la patria mía,
Del sol nacida que me ha dado Dios.

Así en el alta aurora irradial
Punta de flecha el áureo rostro imita,
Y forma estela al purpurado cuello.
El ala es paño, el águila es bandera.

Es la bandera de la patria mía,
Del sol nacida que me ha dado Dios;

Es la bandera de la patria mía,
Del sol nacida que me ha dado Dios.

Aurora (Hymn to the Flag)

High in the sky a warrior eagle,
Bravely rises in triumphant flight,
One wing blue the color of the sky,
One wing blue the color of the sea.

It is the flag of my Fatherland,
Born of the sun given to me by God;
It is the flag of my Fatherland,
Born of the sun given to me by God.

Thus on high radiant aurora
The golden beak imitates the point of the arrow,
And forms a stele to the red-stained neck.
The wing is cloth, the eagle is the flag.

It is the flag of my Fatherland,
Born of the sun given to me by God;

It is the flag of my Fatherland,
Born of the sun given to me by God.

Fernanda García Lao is an Argentine novelist, poet, and playwright, referred to as "the strangest writer of Argentine literature." She was born in Mendoza, Argentina in 1966 to two left-wing journalists, who in 1975 were forced to flee to Spain, where they lived in exile for nearly twenty years. Fernanda received her education in Spain, studying acting, dance, music, and journalism. When she returned to Argentina in the early nineties, she was trained further as an actress, playwright, and director. She is the author of several novels, plays, and one collection of short stories. Her novels and stories have received wide acclaim and accolades, and have been translated into French, Portuguese, and Swiss. At the 2011 Guadalajara Book Fair, Garcia Lao was named one of the "25 Best Kept Secrets of Latin American Literature." This is her first book in English.

Will Vanderhyden is a freelance translator, with an MA in Literary Translation from the University of Rochester. He has translated the work of Carlos Labbé, Rodrigo Fresán, and Fernanda García Lao, among others. His translations have appeared in journals such as *Two Lines*, *The Literary Review*, *The Scofield*, and *The Arkansas International*. He has received fellowships from the NEA and the Lannan Foundation. His translation of *The Invented Part* by Rodrigo Fresán won the 2018 Best Translated Book Award for Fiction.

PARTNERS

pixel ||| texel

<u>ADDITIONAL DONORS</u>, CONT'D

Mark Haber
Mary Cline
Maynard Thomson
Michael Reklis
Mike Soto
Mokhtar Ramadan
Nikki & Dennis Gibson
Patrick Kukucka
Patrick Kutcher
Rev. Elizabeth & Neil Moseley
Richard Meyer

Scott & Katy Nimmons
Sherry Perry
Sydneyann Binion
Stephen Harding
Stephen Williamson
Susan Carp
Susan Ernst
Theater Jones
Tim Perttula
Tony Thomson

SUBSCRIBERS

Ned Russin
Michael Binkley
Michael Schneiderman
Aviya Kushner
Kenneth McClain
Eugenie Cha
Lance Salins
Stephen Fuller
Joseph Rebella
Brian Matthew Kim

Andreea Pritcher
Anthony Brown
Michael Lighty
Kasia Bartoszynska
Erin Kubatzky
Shelby Vincent
Margaret Terwey
Ben Fountain
Caroline West

AVAILABLE NOW FROM DEEP VELLUM

MICHÈLE AUDIN · *One Hundred Twenty-One Days*
translated by Christiana Hills · FRANCE

BAE SUAH · *Recitation*
translated by Deborah Smith · SOUTH KOREA

MARIO BELLATIN · *Mrs. Murakami's Garden*
translated by Heather Cleary · MEXICO

EDUARDO BERTI · *The Imagined Land*
translated by Charlotte Coombe · ARGENTINA

CARMEN BOULLOSA · *Texas: The Great Theft* · *Before* · *Heavens on Earth*
translated by Samantha Schnee · Peter Bush · Shelby Vincent · MEXICO

LEILA S. CHUDORI · *Home*
translated by John H. McGlynn · INDONESIA

SARAH CLEAVE, ed. · *Banthology: Stories from Banned Nations* ·
IRAN, IRAQ, LIBYA, SOMALIA, SUDAN, SYRIA & YEMEN

ANANDA DEVI · *Eve Out of Her Ruins*
translated by Jeffrey Zuckerman · MAURITIUS

ALISA GANIEVA · *Bride and Groom* · *The Mountain and the Wall*
translated by Carol Apollonio · RUSSIA

ANNE GARRÉTA · *Sphinx* · *Not One Day*
translated by Emma Ramadan · FRANCE

JÓN GNARR · *The Indian* · *The Pirate* · *The Outlaw*
translated by Lytton Smith · ICELAND

GOETHE · *The Golden Goblet: Selected Poems* · *Faust, Part One*
translated by Zsuzsanna Ozsváth and Frederick Turner · GERMANY

NOEMI JAFFE · *What are the Blind Men Dreaming?*
translated by Julia Sanches & Ellen Elias-Bursac · BRAZIL

CLAUDIA SALAZAR JIMÉNEZ · *Blood of the Dawn*
translated by Elizabeth Bryer · PERU

JUNG YOUNG MOON · *Seven Samurai Swept Away in a River* · *Vaseline Buddha*
translated by Yewon Jung · SOUTH KOREA

KIM YIDEUM · *Blood Sisters*
translated by Ji yoon Lee · SOUTH KOREA

JOSEFINE KLOUGART · *Of Darkness*
translated by Martin Aitken · DENMARK

YANICK LAHENS · *Moonbath*
translated by Emily Gogolak · HAITI

FOUAD LAROUI · *The Curious Case of Dassoukine's Trousers*
translated by Emma Ramadan · MOROCCO

MARIA GABRIELA LLANSOL · *The Geography of Rebels Trilogy: The Book of Communities;*
The Remaining Life; In the House of July & August
translated by Audrey Young · PORTUGAL

PABLO MARTÍN SÁNCHEZ · *The Anarchist Who Shared My Name*
translated by Jeff Diteman · SPAIN

DOROTA MASŁOWSKA · *Honey, I Killed the Cats*
translated by Benjamin Paloff · POLAND

BRICE MATTHIEUSSENT · *Revenge of the Translator*
translated by Emma Ramadan · FRANCE

LINA MERUANE · *Seeing Red*
translated by Megan McDowell · CHILE

VALÉRIE MRÉJEN · *Black Forest*
translated by Katie Shireen Assef · FRANCE

FISTON MWANZA MUJILA · *Tram 83*
translated by Roland Glasser · DEMOCRATIC REPUBLIC OF CONGO

GORAN PETROVIĆ · *At the Lucky Hand, aka The Sixty-Nine Drawers*
translated by Peter Agnone · SERBIA

ILJA LEONARD PFEIJFFER · *La Superba*
translated by Michele Hutchison · NETHERLANDS

RICARDO PIGLIA · *Target in the Night*
translated by Sergio Waisman · ARGENTINA

SERGIO PITOL · *The Art of Flight* · *The Journey* ·
The Magician of Vienna · *Mephisto's Waltz: Selected Short Stories*
translated by George Henson · MEXICO

EDUARDO RABASA · *A Zero-Sum Game*
translated by Christina MacSweeney · MEXICO

ZAHIA RAHMANI · *"Muslim": A Novel*
translated by Matthew Reeck · FRANCE/ALGERIA

JUAN RULFO · *The Golden Cockerel & Other Writings*
translated by Douglas J. Weatherford · MEXICO

OLEG SENTSOV · *Life Went On Anyway*
translated by Uilleam Blacker · UKRAINE

MIKHAIL SHISHKIN · *Calligraphy Lesson: The Collected Stories*
translated by Marian Schwartz, Leo Shtutin,
Mariya Bashkatova, Sylvia Maizell · RUSSIA

ÓFEIGUR SIGURÐSSON · *Öræfi: The Wasteland*
translated by Lytton Smith · ICELAND

MUSTAFA STITOU · *Two Half Faces*
translated by David Colmer · NETHERLANDS

FORTHCOMING FROM DEEP VELLUM

MAGDA CARNECI · *FEM*
translated by Sean Cotter · ROMANIA

MIRCEA CĂRTĂRESCU · *Solenoid*
translated by Sean Cotter · ROMANIA

MATHILDE CLARK · *Lone Star*
translated by Martin Aitken · DENMARK

LOGEN CURE · *Welcome to Midland: Poems* · USA

PETER DIMOCK · *Daybook from Sheep Meadow* · USA

CLAUDIA ULLOA DONOSO · *Little Bird*, translated by Lily Meyer · PERU/NORWAY

LEYLÂ ERBIL · *A Strange Woman*
translated by Nermin Menemencioğlu · TURKEY

ROSS FARRAR · *Ross Sings Cheree & the Animated Dark: Poems* · USA

FERNANDA GARCIA LAU · *Out of the Cage*
translated by Will Vanderhyden · ARGENTINA

ANNE GARRÉTA · *In/concrete*
translated by Emma Ramadan · FRANCE

JUNG YOUNG MOON · *Arriving in a Thick Fog*
translated by Mah Eunji and Jeffrey Karvonen · SOUTH KOREA

FISTON MWANZA MUJILA · *The Villain's Dance*, translated by Roland Glasser · *The River in the Belly: Selected Poems*, translated by Bret Maney · DEMOCRATIC REPUBLIC OF CONGO

LUDMILLA PETRUSHEVSKAYA · *Kidnapped: A Crime Story*, translated by Marian Schwartz · *The New Adventures of Helen: Magical Tales*, translated by Jane Bugaeva · RUSSIA

JULIE POOLE · *Bright Specimen: Poems from the Texas Herbarium* · USA

MANON STEFAN ROS · *The Blue Book of Nebo* · WALES

ETHAN RUTHERFORD · *Farthest South & Other Stories* · USA

ROBERT TRAMMELL · *Jack Ruby & the Origins of the Avant-Garde in Dallas* · USA